Immortal
Infidel

An Unearthly Child Chronicle 2

Copyright 2011 Leisel

Immortal Infidel

An Unearthly Child Chronicle 2

by

Leisel

Copyright August 2011

All Rights Reserved

Leiselbooks.com

Cover Art and Design by

Courtney Kurtenbach

Thanks to Rachel, Chanel, Michael and Courtney- you make my life complete.

Library of Congress Cataloging in Publication Number: 3674063

ISBN-13: 978-1466242838
ISBN-10: 1466242833

LCCN# 3674063

------------------Contents

Immortal Infidel

Chapter 1

My brothers dead- the evil man said so- but he did speak of another. Gentry couldn't stop thinking about him- *he had said he was the devil, but again he said he was only a monk who had sold his soul- he said plenty of things.*

Ever since Gentry had returned with Katie, her hated sister by adoption, their folks had been deeply suspicious of her. They wondered how did she *know* where to find Katie? Why did Gentry not say where she had been? Even Gentry's father, who had once been the only source of fondness ever received, had become foreign to her. Gentry had decided not to tell the authorities about the evil man just yet. She kept the diary that she had found in the man's castle, the one that told about the horrible deeds he had done. She kept it secret with her, in a secret place, for someday she would have the opportunity to show the world who she had found. That day wasn't today.

Gentry found herself going back to the convent where she had been born. She was riding on her motorcycle with her visor in the down position, going as fast as she could go, for the roads were slippery now that it was December, two weeks till Christmas. She was making the trip because of what the evil man had told her in his presence.. that there was 'another'. Gentry took that to mean that there was another one born when she and her brother were delivered- triplets! She also knew that this baby had to be another girl- like she was, 'useless', according to the evil man. He had waited till the boy was born, then cut the birthing cord with the sharp rock he picked up in the barn.

2

He had to know she was born, had to be born before

the boy- gone just before I was born and just before the

ceiling came down in the fire that destroyed the barn.

What the hell happened to her?

Twilight had just begun when she arrived. She paused

outside the gates and walked around the convent to the

back area and looked over the rubble of the barn, looking

for anything that would tell her about that night. She knew

from the nuns that the fire department never showed, so

there was never an   investigation. The burnt out building

was covered in a light snow, even now it was falling

gently. All she found was burnt out bits of char, lumber

and steel that belonged to tools that were once inside.

Walking around what once was the interior inside, she

had to be careful, for there were pitched roof ceiling slabs

that had once been overhead, and with every step she

risked stepping on an

old, rusty nail or sharp tooling.   She ran her gloved hand over the rubble when she came to a central area of the barn that was blackened, but she realized when she moved the charred pieces away, it was mostly intact- as it had been petrifying for 22 years. She saw the ash outline of a woman, lying on her back with her legs apart, as if in mid-birth. She touched the outline- the ash fell away, and all that were left were bones. Gentry stood there and looked with her mouth agape- this was where she was born- she and her siblings- all those years ago. She picked up the skull, with it's mouth open, the bottom jaw separated from the headpiece as if to scream that what happened here was a true nightmare. Gentry looked at the skull with curiosity, with the tenderest fingers of someone who was looking for the first time.

Yes, there was a huge piece missing on the leftside- just as the nun had told her- her head *had* been bashed in .

Carefully she put the skull into her backpack and zipped it tight- now she would be able to find out about her mother, no matter how much the nuns pleaded ignorance. Shivers went down her spine when she played back the horrors of that night, where she stood, the absolute terror of what happened that night.

Slowly she backed away, coming out in the exact same footprints in which she had entered. Bravely she went up the steps to the convent, ready for another round with the nun who she dealt with before. Gentry took a deep breath and went to push the doorbell as she had before, but now there was a small sign over the button that read 'doorbell broken, ring bell'. There was a circular metal bell that was rigged onto the door. She rang the bell. As before, it was a long while before the door opened. A strange nun answered.

"Yes? What is it ? What do you want?"

"Hello. I was here once before and I spoke with a certain nun. I never got her name, but I'm certain she was the Mother Superior by the way she spoke."

The nun looked Gentry up and down, with a sneer that told her what she thought of her.

"Yes. *I remember you.* The Mother Superior told us all about you. Go Away! We don't need anything *you* have to sell." and she tried to slam the door, but Gentry remembering what happened before had her boot already in the way.

"I had a feeling you would try to keep me out. I'm not going to go until I see that nun! I understand that sister Mary Alice has died already." she said with a certain matter of fact tone in her voice.

"You're too late!" the nun shouted, "Mother Superior is in her death bed. She doesn't have much time left."

"So, you've already called the doctor? Is that what he

6

told you?"

"Of course we didn't call the doctor! We can't afford a doctor! It doesn't take a professional to see what her condition is, she's passing away as we speak."

"You're killing her yourselves?! How can you *not* get a doctor for her? Don't you care about her at all?"

"Go away! Mother Superior called you an unearthly child, that our penance was due because of you! *We all know what you are!*"

Gentry pushed the door open and saw rats scurrying down the hallways, it was worse than before. *Rats!* Gentry hated the disease carrying rodents- the convent air was filled with their stench.

The darkness was pierced by the light of the candle that shone down the entryway. She ran past the candle, there was barely enough light to see, but she could make her way around in the dark. She went up the stairs with the

7

nun carrying the candle behind her, yelling at her to get

out.   The second floor landing stood there before her,

with identical doors right and left, then she saw one

window at the end of the hall that overlooked the area in

in back where the barn had stood, to the left was the last

door and she knew this was *the* door. Gentry threw open

the door and stood in dread of what she saw.

Mother Superior Catherine lay in bed, with the thinnest

sheet over her scrawny body, she lay there emaciated. Her

face looked like a hollowed out, dried up pumpkin. A

tinge of sympathy ran through Gentry's veins, then the

horror when she remembered what they had done to her.

"Catherine? That is you name, isn't it?"

She turned her head slowly towards Gentry, she could

hear her laboring for her to breath, as her breaths were

staccato.

"What do you want?" she half moaned, "Did you come

back to gloat? Did you find him?"

Gentry watched as she lie there shivering. She walked over to the big, broken down chest and pulled out another thin sheet and covered her.

"I don't know who you mean." Gentry said as she lightly sat on the corner of the bed. "I've come back because I have some questions for you to answer. It seems that you were not totally candid with me before. I already know about Sister Mary Alice's death, so please don't try to hide things from me."

The air was filled with the sounds of breathing, slow, hard breathing.

"If you were truly sorry, you wouldn't have come back." she spat. Then she started to violently cough. Gentry reached for the glass of water on her nightstand, then recoiled when she realized it was the green, slimy water that filled the container. Catherine's cough sounded like it

9

was coming from deep in her bowels, though it was weak.

Gentry continued, "I know I have a sister. You didn't tell me everything last time I was here."

"You don't have a sister- I don't know what you're talking about." *cough, cough.*

"The man you believe to be the devil told me I do, *now tell me the truth!"* Gentry's voice was getting more abrupt.

"I don't know what you mean." *cough.*

There in the corner of the room stood her old nemesis, the grim reaper. He wasn't moving, he was merely floating in the darkness- waiting for Catherine to die.

"Why don't you ask her about the key?" he whispered.

"What key?" she whispered back.

"The key that has the answers to your questions- *that* box." he said and then he started laughing that horrible laugh, it was dreadful.

10

"She's going to die now, isn't she?"

"Would you be pleased, or would you regret it?"

Gentry looked at him with her answer written on her face. "Neither. I would have no reaction whatsoever."

"I'll take her shortly. I *love* arriving early; especially when you're here...there aren't many people who amuse me- just a few, really."

"Can you give her enough time to answer my questions? Can you?"

"If I give you favors, people will begin to talk about *us!*" he began laughing again. "No, really- I could give you a moment or two- but do you really think she will answer your questions?"

"She must!"

Catherine thought that Gentry was talking to her, and it confused what was left of her mind,

"Leave me, leave me now!"

"Catherine, I know that I had a sister- did you put her up for adoption as well?"

"I don't know what you're talking about- and even if I did, why would I ever tell you?" *cough.*

"She's got but a minute- hurry and get your answers!" the grim reaper said aloud.

Cough, cough...cough....

"What about the key? Tell me where it is, what am I looking for?" Gentry's fingers were clenched tight in her gloves. Then her hand went up to Catherine's neck, she had on an old, frilly frock, with lace about the neck- there! She had a necklace with a key!

"I found it! I found the key!" she was excited to a fault. "What does this belong to? Catherine, Catherine!"

Catherine pointed with her bony finger towards the closet and said, "She lives here- she's always lived here...." then the grim reaper took Catherine's sad life. He

12

threw his black cape around Catherine and said, "See you later." sounding to a deep guttural laugh.

Gentry was alone once again. She was sure the other nuns were just behind the door, she was sure that the nun who let her in had gone down and rounded up the crew- very soon they would be coming in- so Gentry quickly took the necklace off Catherine and put it in her pocket. Now she had to locate what it belonged to- so she took a look in the closet, *not there.* She looked in her nightstand, *not there.* Finally she looked under her bed- There were tons of crucifixes, and so much dust she thought she would choke. *There!* Here was a box with a lock- this had to be it- *Damn the grim reaper, why can't he tell me what I want to know? Goddamn him!!*

The room was getting darker, and the light from the candle was starting to burn out.

She looked back at Catherine, she had been alive

moments ago. Her face withered down, like a balloon that had been popped; Gentry felt bad for her, for only for a moment.

I'm sorry Catherine, sorry that you're dead, and sorry that as much pleasure as it gave you, you won't have me to piss around with anymore!

Suddenly she heard the nuns knocking on the door.

"Mother Superior! Mother Superior please may we open the door?!"

Gentry sat with her back against the door to block the sisters from coming in while she sat with the metal box on her lap. She slipped the key inside the lock- it didn't fit. Vainly she pulled on the lock, hoping for a miracle. It worked! The locked pulled open to Gentry's excitement. She immediately opened the metal box, hoping it would tell her anything about her sister. All she found were super 8 films and underneath a small diary.

14

It must have been kept by Mary Alice, or Catherine- or both!

Gentry carefully opened the diary- the writing of the first pages was too old to read- but she could read what was on the later pages. It was a chronograph of meal service, that's all.

Gentry put the lock back on and stood up, she opened the door.

"You dreadful girl! You are a sorry piece of garbage." the nun spat as she rushed to Catherine's side and held her wrist to check for a pulse.

"Don't bother- she's dead."

"What did you do to her? You frightened our dear Mother Catherine away!" the nun began to cry.

"I did no such thing! Maybe she died because of the pneumonia she had, huh? You could hear it in her breathing, you knew she was going to die whether I was

15

here or not."

"Where did you get that box?" another sister demanded to know. "Did you get it from her?" Suddenly there were five nuns in the room.

"She said I could have it before she died. I *am* taking it with me."

The sisters all started crying and wailing around Catherine's body. "You are an unholy child of Satan! Leave us to bury our dead."

"*No problem!* I'm out of here."

Gentry turned to leave the premises when she saw a nun standing at the end of the hallway, holding a candle. She had an eerie glow about her. She was beckoning to her. Gentry assessed the nun, small like the others, but she was at least 40 years younger than the rest. She couldn't tell what color was her hair was- as she had on her habit- most of the nuns wore them- but not all. But she was trained in

16

recognizing individuals and she could see that dark brown eyebrows and lightness of skin that she was a true European by blood, and when she heard her speak- her accent confirmed what she had suspected.

When Gentry reached her she took her arm and led her down into the chapel- a part of the convent that up till now she had not seen. It was cramped, only four pews deep with a huge statue of Christ at the other end.

"We can talk here." the nun whispered.

"What?" Gentry said severely.

"I do not know how to ask you...I do not know how."

"Ask me what?" Gentry threw the sisters arms off her then grabbed the nun by the shoulders. "Have you seen my sister- I mean my *real* sister. She was born here at the same time I was, she and my brother." If anyone had seen her, you might be the one.

"No, I have not. I have seen only what you have

seen yourself. No, what I want to tell you is that I am frightened, most dreadfully frightened. I do no wish to be here- there are ghosts here!" She was shaking.

"Ghosts? You think you have ghosts here?" Gentry relaxed her grip.

"Yes! I hear them in the walls at night. I hear them whistle all the time. Wait! Hear that? Wasn't that a whistle?" she was looking all around at the walls.

"I don't think that they'll hurt you. *If* you do have ghosts, they're probably noisemakers- kind of like poltergeists."

"Poltergeists?"

"Not like that. I don't mean like the movies- poltergeists is the German word for ghosts that make clatter-noise- that's all."

"Oh." the sister said with relief in her voice, "but that does not make any difference. I do not want to be in this convent- I am tired of being destitute; poor I can well

18

imagine, poor is what I counted on- destitute is not! And certainly not destitute with ghosts!" her eyes were hard for Gentry to read as it was dark, but even she knew that they were filled with tears.

"The other sisters do not talk to me, I am new blood. They keep secrets, they do not talk in my presence- they ignore me- it's as if I do not exist! Won't you please take me with you?" she pleaded.

Gentry listed off the reasons *not* to take her. "I came on my motorcycle, I don't have a helmet for you to wear, it's freezing outside- and it's dark!"

"Please help me escape; please, please help me!!" her tears were heart wrenching.

"Where would I take you?"

"Take me anywhere- anywhere is better than here."

Gentry certainly couldn't argue with what she said, anywhere would be better.

19

"I suppose I could take you to my house for tonight. Tomorrow I can take you to the shelter for battered women- you appear battered to me."

"Oh thank you so much, thank you!" she started kissing Gentry's gloved hands.

In Catherine's bedroom Gentry could hear the rest of the convent wailing over her death bed. She took this as her clue to disappear. Sneaking out the back door of the chapel Gentry had to have the sister help her move two large iron rods, left from days of construction, away from the door so they could make their escape.

"Do not worry about setting off the alarm, it has been broken for years." the nun whispered.

"These rods are heavy, can you help me move them away from the door?" Gentry asked, the nun nodded as they worked to move the iron rods to lean on the back wall. They opened the back door and ran towards her

20

motorcycle. Through the swirling snow all you could hear was their crunchy footsteps running away. Then, suddenly there was a faint whistle. The nun said, "Did you not hear that? It is that whistle again! It is going to start again. The walls are going to come alive in a moment!"

Gentry *did* hear a slight whistle, and she stopped for a moment and looked back at the convent. *I'm hearing things. It's probably the pipes...*

"What will they do when they find the irons moved and you gone?"

"I am not sure exactly. They will probably assume I had left them- or they might decided you kidnapped me- either way, they will not call anyone- they cannot- they do not have a working phone."

Huh! There are more and more monsters here than I presumed. I don't think it's on purpose, but they are worse than the devil they were trying to protect me from.

21

"I believe I'm doing a good thing by taking you away. They are monsters. I don't even know what all they did, but I do know it had to be ghastly!" Gentry started her bike and gestured for the nun to join her.

"Hold on tight!" Gentry said as she turned the corner hard and rode away. She could feel the nun shivering on the back seat, huddling with her arms crushing her. She pulled off the road when they were out of sight of the convent and Gentry gave the nun her jacket.

"What are you doing? You are *not* giving me *your* jacket?" the nun looked confused.

"Just take it." she tried not to sound too tender. She didn't want to give the air of comfort- or condemnation.

"You are being so kind to me- especially when you feel about the nuns the way you do."

"You're the one who wants to run away from them. You can't be all bad."

22

They rode in silence the rest of the way back to Gentry's house. They pulled in around the back of the house as to not wake her parents. As they got off the motorcycle Gentry told the nun to be silent as they entered the house.

"I don't think they'd be awake right now, but you never know."

They slipped inside the house to Gentry's room at the far corner of the dwelling. She started talking.

"Okay. You're safe now. What the hell is your name? Don't give me that bullshit nuns name- but your *real* name?"

"I haven't spoken that name for years- it feels like I'm committing a sin if I tell you."

"YOU ARE NOT committing a sin. You're done with that life."

The nun shifted from one foot to the other. She gave a modest little sigh and said, "My name is Jecka."

23

"Jecka? Huh." Gentry said. She was tired, and amazed that the grim reaper was there to take Catherine's life. *He always does that! Surprise me by showing up when I don't expect him. I suppose that's why I had him tattooed on my back!* For Gentry had the reaper tattooed on her back, along with a laundry list of other tattoos on her body. She had the dark look of a Gothic, or Goths that was seen in the area. She had a tortured soul that no one seemed to care about, apart from her one friend Bryce, whom she cared for with her seemingly rough exterior, but who's crumbling interior she hid well.

Chapter 2

"Here. Put these on." she threw Jecka some pants from her drawer and a sweater, both black. "Get out of those clothes, it makes me sick just looking at them."

"Thank you so much." Jeka said, "These old clothes were all they had to give me to wear. I am so grateful to be out of there."

"I have my own bathroom, it's thru there; go and change- then come back- I need to ask you some serious questions." Gentry said as she threw herself onto the bed.

When Jecka came out of the bathroom dresses in black clothes she took on the unreal air of being a normal person. She took a seat in the chair that was over by the closed door.

"We won't disturb your parents?"

"Not after they go to bed. I don't think we'll disturb

Katie, either- the folks give her a giant sleeping pill- as prescribed by the doctor- ever since she came back. She has 'dreams'." she said as she covered her eyes with her hands. "She would wake up screaming."

"Where did she come back from?" Jecka asked.

"That's the question, now- isn't it?" an eerie silence came between them. "She was kidnapped."

"Kidnapped? By whom?" Jecka was astonished, "That's awful!"

"Yeah, sure. It was horrible for her." Gentry said not sounding particularly horrified. "I want to ask you about life in the convent. If anyone knew what was going on, it should be you- you lived there."

"What do you want to know? It was dreadful in there- we had no light, other than candles- we didn't even have clean water."

"I want to know about Catherine and her whereabouts. I

26

knew that Mary Alice has died already, so we can cross her off the list."

"I have told you already, they did not talk to me. All I had to do all day was work in the garden to get food out of the ground, when it was nice enough to get food out of the ground- give the animals water, you know, try to stay occupied- idle hands are the devils workshop." Jecka replied as she grabbed for a blanket on Gentry's bed. "Do you mind if I use this? It's nice to be in a warm house."

"Take it." she answered, "I think that Mary Alice and Catherine were involved together in a plot to take care of a baby- now she would be as old as me."

"I have no knowledge of any plot- sister Mary Alice was kind of..." she paused.

"Demented. I know how she was."

"Yes. She was demented. But she did have times when she was remarkably coherent. She was also, blind- as you

27

already know."

"I knew."

"You know what they called you?"

"Yes. When I was leaving the last time they were calling out that I was an unearthly child. I suppose you know why?" Gentry leaned forward.

"No. They never explained why- they just said that you were evil, that we were not to talk to you-ever." she shivered in her blanket.

"But you did talk to me- you even asked me if I would get you out of that place- aren't you afraid of burning in hell?"

"No! I am not. I could not believe the things they told me; no more! They might have said you were the devil incarnate- I do not believe in God anymore. If there was a God, he would not have put me in that place. There is no god- there is only the devil, of that I am sure." Jecka

28

lowered her head and pulled the blanket until she was completely covered.

"Jecka," Gentry began, "I need you to put aside your beliefs for a moment- okay?"

She nodded her head.

"Catherine is dead, and Mary Alice has been dead for weeks now- do you know what this is?" She pushed the metal box towards her. Jecka looked at the box with innocence reflected in her eyes. She shook her head and said, "No. I have no idea."

"Did they ever tell you about the barn that burned out back?"

"No. I assumed that it had burned down long before I arrived, and since no one told me about it, I never asked. They were precise on that point- when I arrived they told me not to ask questions- about anything."

"Shit!" Gentry whispered.

29

"You have not asked me about the ghosts. That is what I could not take- the frightening ghosts."

Gentry knew that ghosts had been here on Earth since the beginning of time, some of the time they spoke, other times they would be seen; but only by the chosen few. Some people preyed on willing participants, saying that they saw ghosts and could communicate with them- for a price- taking advantage of their naivete. The rest of the population scoffed, turning up their noses at the whole idea of ghosts. Gentry wasn't sure what category Jecka fell into; maybe she was hearing the wind through the creaky boards at the convent- it was old and needed new roofing and countless other things- but she would give her the benefit of the doubt.

"Tell me about the ghosts, Jecka. Tell me."

"Ever since I arrived there I heard a pounding on the walls and always at mealtime. Other times I would hear a

30

whistle. Both sounds were bone chilling." she began, "I thought that it was evil spirits, since every other thing that had to do with the convent was evil. I thought this was sent from hell, as well. The rats- oh, the rats..."

"I know about the rats." Gentry said with empathy, "Go on, tell me more about the ghosts."

"Sometimes when I was lying in bed, trying to get warm, I would hear the whistle- it was a single note, and it would only go off every once in a while. I would be so happy when I didn't hear it- even though I was cold to my bones."

"Go on." Gentry prodded.

"When the one note would stop the pounding on the walls would begin. It was a loud, *thump, thump, thump!* Then it would stop. It was eerie, *dreadfully eerie."* Jecka whispered the last part, her head hanging low. "It was almost like it was trying to tell us a secret... but I could

31

never figure out that that was. I would pray for it to go away, but it got louder and more frequent. I had to get out of there before I actually started to see things- it is one thing to hear ghosts, but it is quite another to *see ghosts.* "

"Have you ever seen a ghost, Jecka?"

"Yes. In my old country."

"Where are you from?"

"A small village in Romania- you might call it Transylvania. It is on the border, on the Carpathian mountains. It has been one country or another over time depending on who won the the latest war. Yes, I saw evil entities walking the dark forests at night." she slowly continued, "I do not mean *vampires.* That is a delusion that had been around for ages- even I am not that superstitious- they are *not* real."

"But you saw ghosts- did you ever talk to one of them?"

"Of course not. Why would I try? No, no...it is better to

get away from them...do not talk to ghosts, for they are devils spawn- they can only *lie* to you...they would never tell you the truth."

"So what happened, did you try to get away from them by coming to this country?"

"My brother came here first. He working his way up from a simple embalmer to a full fledged mortician. He started buying up run down mortuary's across the state...not this state, of course. Then he could afford to bring my mother and me to the states. Of course we were happy to leave the old country and come to America. We came here and were happy living with my brother for about a year, then the 'bad' thing happened." her eyes glazed over.

"Explain."

"He was possessed! He came home from work one night and started fighting with mother. I was in my bedroom,

33

but I could not help but hear them arguing. It became violent and I heard a lamp shatter, then I heard a gunshot- I ran out to see what happened."

"Which was..."

"He was standing there covered in blood, my mother's blood. I was suddenly afraid he would shoot me- but I asked him what he had done to mother- then he pointed the gun into his mouth, I screamed for him to stop- by then he pulled the trigger and it blew half of his head away, then his body fell. I was watching this happen in slow motion. I screamed and screamed and it took five minutes for the police to come, but it seemed more like 5 years. The neighbors must have called the police when they heard the gunshots...I don't know who or what happened after that except that I found out something had gone wrong with the money that day...that my brother was wiped out financially. I have my guess as to what

34

happened- I suppose he wanted to wipe out the family so he wouldn't be embarrassed in our mother's eyes." Jecka stopped.

"Cheese and crackers! Holy fucking shit! Is that why you joined the convent?" She nodded.

"On the day of the funerals, a nun came up to me and told me that if I didn't have a place to go that I could join their convent and find peace. Ha! Peace. All I found was a living hell." Jecka was shivering despite the blanket wrapped round her body. "At night, when I dream,I find myself standing in pools of blood...buckets of blood. I find that I cannot sleep. After that there were mornings when I got up earlier than 5- which is the normal time we woke at the convent- I would walk around the grounds of the convent, in warmer weather of course. On those days, I could have sworn I saw a little ghost wandering the grounds- hiding behind the trees, watching me."

"How did you know it was a ghost?" her interest aroused once more.

"Because I could swear that I saw the ghost walking thru the trees, just as they did back home.

"Did you try to call the ghost?"

"NO! I told you, if you see a ghost you must not try to make communications with it- I did not want to burn in hell for doing that."

"What did it look like?"

"As I said, it was a small ghost. Probably the ghost of a little girl. She wore a sack cloth for a dress that came down to it's ankle's, and it wore socks with those little black shoes that had the strap over the top. But what stuck me the most, I mean I was actually scared by this- was the little hood that came down to it's shoulders- I could tell the head was misshapen because it was wasn't round, it was flat on one side- almost as if it had been cut down the

36

middle. There was a small hole cut for where the mouth would be- it was truly a terror to behold. I dream about it still- or should I say I still have nightmares?" Jecka was shaking still.

"So this was *the* ghost you've seen at the convent, am I correct?"

"Correct, but as I said, I do *not* forget to run from a ghost, not run too."

"Was anyone else awake? No other nuns?"

"No. I was the only one awake, I'm sure of that."

"Wow. I guess I can only say thank you, Jecka. I'm going to have to find out more, but I can safely say that it won't be from you." Gentry rolled over in her bed and stood up. "Why don't you sleep in my bed tonight? I'm going to sleep on the chair."

"Are you sure? I am perfectly comfortable here- it's already more plush than where I am used to sleeping, you have heat, at least."

"I'm sure. There are things I have to decipher. I'll probably be awake all night."

"One more favor, if I may ask?" Jecka said almost inaudibly.

"What's that?"

"Could I possibly get some food and water? I hate to ask, but it was rat eaten bread and putrid water for so long...." her voice trailed off.

"I totally forget about what I brought you from, the convent- the hell hole." Gentry stood up and hit her forehead with the butt of her hand. "Of course I'll get you food and water. Wait here."

Chapter 3

While she was in the kitchen, images were swirling round Gentry's head. Jecka had seen a ghost, but what kind of ghost? Was it the type she had seen in Romania? Gentry wasn't even sure that they were *real*. But to people who came from Romania, they *were* real. She wanted to ask Jeka about that, but first she wanted to ask her about the charm that came from the evil man.

"That would freak anyone out- including me." she had said to herself.

Suddenly, out of the darkness came a familiar voice- Katies'. "What does that mean, 'that would freak anyone out?'"

"Katie! You surprised me- I didn't expect you there- what are you doing up? Shouldn't you be in bed?"

"Wandering. How about you?" she said with the vacant stare of heavy medication.

"Hungry."

Katie stared at Gentry, like she was in a trance. Gentry's palms started to sweat.

"Katie," Gentry said to awaken her, "You really should get back to bed. You look exhausted."

"You'd be exhausted too if you had the nightmares I have." she said in a monotone voice.

"What nightmares do you mean?" She tried to sound like she didn't know what Katie meant. But Gentry knew.

"I'm going to go back to bed now." Katie said as she turned to walk away. Gentry was relived, although she didn't know how she felt about Katie now. Her feelings vacillated between hate and sorrow- although most of the time, hate had the greater edge.

Gentry had put together a pastrami sandwich and a glass of soy milk for Jecka, and a cup of hot cocoa for herself.

"This feast is for me?" Jecka's mouth fell open.

"Of course. What did you think I would bring?"

"If it was anything like the convent, I guess stale crackers and putrid water. This is *so* much! Thank you." she said as she hungrily picked up the sandwich and dove right in. Gentry decided to ask her about the charm.

"Jecka?"

"Um hm?" she tried to talk with her mouth full.

"Have you ever seen this? It's a charm, it's very old."

She slowly nodded her head.

"This is a charm that is supposedly to keep evil spirits away- look, there's a small Romanian saying here on the talisman."

"Oh?" Gentry had never noticed this before.

"People claim that they are vampires; and you know that you have to be dead to be a vampire." she dramatically said.

"It says *Death comes to the damned.*" Jecka said in a

shuddered voice.

"I do not like this. Here." Jecka shoved the charm back into Gentry's hands.

"What does the saying mean to you?"

"It is a warning. I do not believe in going against talismans such as these. I do not want to believe in monsters and such."

"Okay, I'm not saying that you have to believe."

"Good. Because I know there are other monsters." she stopped, then continued.

"Oh yes. There are creatures that would curl your hair." Jecka said in her most deadpan voice.

Gentry picked up the blanket on the empty chair and cuddled down. She was ready to hear about *immortals*.

Jecka told Gentry some of the tales that come from her old country- and they were ghastly. One of the stories she told her was about a young man who was getting engaged to a young woman of no consequence- she had no money and he, of course was wealthy. He knew that his father would object to their marriage, so he kept it quiet as long as he could. But talk was fierce and word got back to the father that his son had asked for her hand in marriage. This enraged the father and he called for the young woman to come and see him. When she at last was in his presence he demanded to know if indeed his son had asked for her hand- and she shyly said, yes- it was true. This pushed the father over the edge and he turned into a werewolf and devoured the young woman, except for her hand.

When he turned back into his old body he realized what had happened, but still he could not accept that his son would marry such a girl. So he put her hand into a box and sent it to his son. When his son received the box he anxiously opened it- only to find her hand, the one with

43

the ring he had given her to be the contents. The son

wailed and suspected his father and confronted him. The

father said, yes, he had done this to the woman, and he

was not sorry. Now the son became enraged and tried to

attack his father, but his father quickly turned into a

werewolf, once again and killed his son. When he came to

he was in shock, he could not believe what he had done to

his son. The father buried his son, with the hand of the

woman and left it at that. But, that was not what their

ghosts wanted, they wanted revenge. So, every night,

when the moon twinkled, they would reunite as lovers and

play ghastly jokes on the father. For the rest of his life he

regretted his decision not to let them marry, but the

revengeful ghosts would not be swayed. They had scared

the servants away, that was easy. Some times they would

wait till he was at the top of the stairs when they would

jump out of nowhere and scream as only a ghost can

scream, and knocked him down the stairs. Other times they would appear at the foot of his bed, joined in hands and they would laugh at him for thinking that he could destroy their love. Finally, this was too much for the old man to take, and he decided to take his life by jumping out of the his window. But he did not count on the lovers making a combined net out of their bodies to stop him from killing himself. When he tried to hang himself the ghosts cut the rope from above. The ghosts would always have the last laugh- and they kept him alive for 50 years making sure that every day, he thought about his son and would be daughter in law, and the love that he could not destroy. ....

"That is only *one* story I have. I know many more." Jecka said looking like she feared them.

"You don't believe them, do you? I mean, werewolves- come on!" Gentry snorted a laugh.

45

"There a many strange things in this world that I do not expect you to believe- but I grew up with stories like that. I *do* believe in them. I believe that ghosts would avenge themselves like that- that they will make themselves heard."

"So you know this charm comes from Romania?" she asked this time with a note of sincerity.

"Yes. I believe in them like I believe in ghosts- those of which I *have* seen."

Gentry thought for a moment. Was there anything beyond what she had seen in her life? If so, why aren't they believed in this country like they are in Romania? But then again- there are animals that appear like the Coelacanth, the fish that was supposed to be extinct- then found one day in a fisherman's net- perhaps she was telling the truth. Gentry finally decided that at least she *believed* she was telling the truth- as far as she knew.

46

Chapter 4

Gentry had pulled Q's number out of her jeans. She now held it in her hands. They had exchanged numbers when they were in the hospital and he was getting his head bandaged, also waiting to see how Katie was doing.

"I don't know why we're even exchanging numbers," Q said, "we don't have things to talk about- I don't think I even want to know about what happened on that island-it was weird!"

"I know what you mean- but there might be some things I need to know about;" she stood on her feet exchanging one foot for the other, "I want to forget, too." she lied.

So Q reluctantly gave her his phone number and she gave him hers.

"I want you to know this-" He began, "I won't forget you, I mean, how could I forget you?" he mumbled off.

47

"I've gotta go, police are hanging all over this place- its time for me to get gone!" he said as he pulled his hoodie over the bandages.

"Thanks for *this*." he said as he motioned to his head.

"It was my fault, after all. Thanks for coming back for me-for all the things you did."

"We're cool- k?" he said as he put his fingers up for a peace sign. Gentry gave him a peace sign in return- then watched him fade away into the night.

....

That was two weeks ago, and she had not called him since they parted. But, he hadn't called her either. Gentry crumpled the number in her hand and threw it into the corner of her room and pulled her pillow over her head. *Fuck him if he doesn't call!*

....

It was the following week when she finally picked up the

crumpled ball of paper and dialed his number. It went straight to messages.

"Hey Q," she started a hurried message, "It's me, Gentry. Just wanted to know how your head is doing-gotta go." then she hurriedly hung up. She didn't know what she was going to tell him- she knew he wouldn't want to hear about how the police showed up at the hospital immediately after he left- nor would he want to know about how her parents came down when she called them and told them that she had found Katie. Between her parents and the cops, she wouldn't let anyone in on where she found Katie; Katie would have to tell them herself, if she could ever remember where she had been.

Like a nightmare, she *remembered* what happened that night.

"But tell us *where* you found her!" Ella screamed , she wasn't even trying to keep calm.

49

"Ella," Jack began, "keep your voice down. We agreed *not* to take this out on Gentry."

"I know, I know..."Ella ran on, "but she knows where she found her- she had to know details. I want to know *how* you found my baby, Gentry! HOW?!"

"I followed the trail, mom. I just followed the trail the kidnappers left. They left some dirt from their shoes and I had it analyzed at the university; it was a red clay that is known to come from this area- that's how I knew where to look for clues- honest!" she lied.

"But the police didn't even have *that* clue- and you swoop in and pick her up like she was a bag of laundry? Impossible!"

"The police could have found her just as easily- the cops that came to our house didn't so much as look at her room before they said she was a runaway." Gentry sounded like she was making sense.

50

"She's right, Ella. The police labeled Katie a runaway. Let's leave it- you've got your Katie back- for God's sake, let's be grateful! We should be thanking Gentry- not crucifying her!"

Thanks for that, dad.

"Sir," the officer asked Jack, "Did the police really label your daughter a runaway without doing a thorough check?"

"Yes, they did! They were lazy, no good..."Ella started to scream again.

"ELLA!" Jack did what he *never* did- he interrupted Ella. "You are being less than helpful. Would you please go see to Katie and make sure she's being taken care of- and I will answer the officer's questions."

Ella's mouth fell open. She was in temporary shock. First her precious daughter is kidnapped- then her husband talked back to her. Surely this was a nightmare and she

51

would wake up soon. Ella got up to leave, then she whispered to Gentry, "I am going to get to the bottom of this missy. Don't think you're off the hook."

"ELLA!" Jack said as he pulled her halfway down the hall.

"Maybe you could answer some questions for me?" a lady dressed in clothes that were obvious designer knockoffs asked Gentry. Her brows furrowed.

"Who are you?" Gentry asked.

"My name is Dr. Glen, I'm a psychiatrist on the Seattle police force."

"I don't know anything. I've had a traumatic experience tonight, see here?" she pointed to her head, to her bandages.

"So, that's how you're going to play it?" Dr. Glen asked.

"You're exactly right."

"I *will* be calling on you in the future. We need to talk."

That was how they left things, the police were just as curious as Ella, but they were questions that had to be revisited. Gentry knew that her mom had questions, but she wasn't asking because she had her beloved Katie back. She knew that Jack had to be curious as well, he knew she didn't find Katie because of some dirt left at the scene. Not that this wasn't possible, but he thought that what he saw was not probable and made him uneasy-*like she was lying?* Gentry knew she had limited time before questions were asked of her. Perhaps that's why she called Q. She knew that he didn't want to be reminded about what happened, but she had questions of her own.

What happened at the castle after they left? Had the police ever even checked the castle? She knew that part of the castle was burned, but why was there no fire department call? Gentry knew that Q was still going to that side of the island because of his smuggling, but she had to know the truth about what happened that night.

Chapter 5

Q stared at his phone, he had just listened to Gentry's message. There was part of him that wanted to call her ever since he had left her at the hospital. Then there was the part of him that wanted nothing more to do with her- she was too close to the police, at least they were close to her. Bringing back her sister wasn't a good thing if you wanted to stay away from the cops. So far the police hadn't pulled him in for questioning- good thing. But now Gentry wanted him to call her- should he? He shoved the phone back into his pocket for now- if he waited a few more days, then he called her, the heat should be off.

After a week Q dialed into his phone Gentry's number. It rang and rang-no answer. Q decided to leave a quick message, "Hey, it's me. I don't know if you're not talking to me or just left your phone. Call me, if you want."

Gentry wasn't answering his call. Maybe if he'd called

sooner- but REALLY? *Muth-a fuck-er!*

After a week had passed, Gentry's anger had passed and she dialed his number and this time he picked it on the first ring.

"Hey! I didn't think you would return my call- maybe that's my fault." he started.

"It's alright." she wasn't sure what she wanted to say, "how's your head?" that should make the call sound official.

"Okay. I wasn't sure I wanted to talk to you."

"Me neither." she had an awkward pause, then continued. "So your head is coming along fine? No aftereffects?"

"The bandages came off after a couple of days. No residual effects. How's what's her name?"

"Katie?"

"Yeah, the wicked Katie."

"She's doing okay. I guess as well as can be expected."

58

"So, my head's ok, Katie's fine- now tell me, what do you want?" he tried to sound hard and cynical.

"I don't want anything, jerk! I wanted to talk to you- don't ask me why!" she slammed the phone in his ear. This whole thing was a mistake.

That piece of shit doesn't want my company- fine!

Gentry threw her phone across the room into the laundry hamper, it rang. Slowly she picked it up, still angry from before- it was Q.

"Don't hang up!" he anxiously said.

"Why shouldn't I? What could you possibly have to say to me now?"

"You're right- I'm sorry! I shouldn't have treated you like that- if anything I should be thanking you."

"For what?" she was still angry.

"For whatever it was that had us in that castle. I don't know, things I never dreamed of were there- I still have

59

problems with the nightmare I had that night. But you kept your head about you- I think it was because of you that we got out of there." Q sounded sincere.

"No, Q- it was because of *you* that we got out of there- I owe you an apology." her anger subsided.

"So we owe each other an apology. How about you come down to Seattle and I take you out for dinner?"

"Dinner? No, that's not why I called."

"Why did you call?" he was suspicious again.

"I wanted to hear you talk; I have questions about that night as well. Plus, it's cool to hear your voice."

"It's good to hear yours, too."

"Q?" Gentry tried to sound like girls sounded in school.

"Yes?"

"I need to talk to you in person- but none of this 'dinner' talk. If I come down to Seattle to see you, it's you I want to see, comprende?"

60

"When do you think you'll be here?"

"I can be there on Saturday, in the late afternoon. Can you see me then?"

"I suppose. You want to meet me in front of Pier 55?"

She was silent. This was the Pier for Blake island, she didn't know if he was kidding or not. "Pier 55?"

"Yeah, I know it's the one for Blake island- it's just easy for you to find, that's all. We don't have to go to Blake island."

"Okay. See you then, late afternoon." she hung up the phone. It was a bit strange, like she was almost looking forward to Saturday.

Chapter 6

"Jecka?" Gentry asked slowly as an idea came into her head, "I have a friend named Bryce who is coming over tomorrow- how would you like to live with her for awhile?"

"Can I not stay with you?" she asked.

"Well, I can't hide you here forever. My folks would freak if they knew you were here."

"Well, if she's a friend of yours, I'm sure I will like her."

"She's nothing like me, actually. She's a bit rough around the edges, but she speaks her mind- if she does not like you, she'll tell you right out. Also, she's been a good friend to me- I think she'll take you in."

Jecka thought for a moment. She wasn't sure that being utterly candid with people was a good idea.

"What happens if she does not like me?"

"Oh, I think she will. Let's not tell her where I picked

you up though, okay?"

"She is not Catholic, I presume?"

"That's right, I'm not sure she's anything." Gentry paused, "And she's disabled."

"Disabled?"

"She was in a terrible car crash a couple years ago- I count myself lucky, actually- I should have been with her when it happened, but I wasn't. I should be crippled myself- or dead."

"You? Why should you have been with her?" Jecka asked.

"It's a long story, but to make it short, she had made plans to take a car trip, a kind of graduation present- her, her cousin and me; we were going to drive down to San Francisco, but at the last minute I didn't go. I understand that they had the music on loud, they were singing and texting and doing everything *but* paying attention to the

64

road and that's when they hit an oncoming car on the highway." Gentry sadly interred, then continued, "Her cousin was killed instantly- she was decapitated. And what's truly awful is that they killed a little girl in the oncoming car- the family's only child. Everyone was touched by that accident, in a terrible way. Bryce's family had a two-fer, her cousin was dead, Bryce was crippled and the other family lost their only child- a gruesome day."

"You called her Bryce?"

"Yes, that's her name."

"I would say Bryce has a lot to be thankful for." Jecka said as she looked towards the heavens.

"Yeah, that's just what she doesn't want to hear. So for my sake, and yours, don't look at her wheelchair and think of her being a cripple, okay?" I think she does not want to have any memories of that night, we all have things about that night that we don't want exposed." Gentry was looking right through Jecka.

"So I have to pretend to ignore the wheelchair?" Jecka asked.

"Yes, ignore the wheelchair. I do think she'll like you, however."

"Why? Why would she like me?"

"Because you sound *foreign.* I believe she likes foreign movies and music. I think it will be good for her to have you around."

"So she does not live with family?"

"No. She wants to be independent. She's always wanted independence. She works at the University, and she's getting her bachelors in early childhood education."

"Alright. If you say to ignore the wheelchair and pretend not to be Catholic, I will try."

"Good." Gentry said as she was spinning around in her

head the idea that she could keep Jecka close, and find out more about life in the convent.

....

The following morning it was snow flurries once more. Jecka still had the blanket wrapped around her even though she had been completely warm the previous night. Gentry stretched and got up from the sofa where she had fallen asleep with her suspicions.

"Good morning Miss Gentry." Jecka was sleepy, but to her it was miraculous to wake in the morning and not be chilled to the bone.

"Let's not have any of that 'Miss' business, okay? Bryce will see through that in a second."

"It is going to hard to pretend *not* to be a nun when you have been nothing else for the past five years."

"Shhhhh." warned Gentry, "I don't want members of my family hearing you either- it would be difficult to

67

explain. Call me G."

"Miss- G?"

"Yeah?"

"Do you think we might have a little something to eat? I hate to bother you, but my stomach is growling like a wolf."

"Sure. Be right back."

Once Jecka had Gentry out of the room she wrapped herself tightly in her blanket and gave thanks to the lord for her rescue, and her rescuer. It was wonderful to be in a warm house with enough food and water to drink- all the creature comforts she had longed for the past five years. Yes, she would be grateful and not tell Bryce that she was a nun, but it was harder to pretend that she did NOT love, in a sisterly way, Gentry. After her prayers, she got up to put on her shoes when Gentry walked back into the room.

"Good," Gentry said, "Bryce should be here soon. Here's

another sandwich and cocoa, and when you're done, look through my closet and see if there's any clothes that fit you- let's get you looking like you're from the real world."

The sandwich was spectacular and the cocoa was hot; she ate and savored the meal.

"Have you thought of becoming a chef, G?"

"Me? Noooooo."

"You make a great sandwich."

"I think that's because you haven't had a decent meal like in forever."

Jecka had barely finished when they heard Bryce's van roll up the driveway.

"How does she drive if she's disabled?"

"She had the gas peddle and brakes worked onto the steering wheel."

"I didn't know they could do that."

"Yeah, it's miraculous the things they do. That's why she

doesn't want the sympathy thing- remember?"

"I will try."

"Okay," Gentry announced, "remember, I found you in the park, you didn't have a place to go- I think she'll buy that."

"Seriously, I will try."

Just then Bryce came bounding in her wheelchair through the door with a smile that lit up the room.

"Hey G! How you doing, girlfriend?"

"I'm good, Bryce."

Bryce noticed the girl in the corner, standing there, looking at her.

"Who's the geek?" Bryce said, Jecka was mortified.

"Gee, Bryce," Gentry started, "I was hoping for a favor today." Gentry coughed a little, "Bryce, this is Jecka. She spent the night here last night."

"Oh?" Bryce's eyebrow went up in one corner.

70

"Nothing like that. I found her in the park, wrapped in a flimsy blanket- she doesn't have anyplace to go- I was hoping she could stay with you for awhile?"

"What?!" Bryce demanded to know, "What's going on?"

"Oh, I would stay out of your way- I promise!" Jecka said using her thickest Romanian accent.

"You're foreign, I take from your accent. I don't get this."

"Bryce," Gentry started again, 'I would let her stay here, but you know how my folks are about me right now- they would never allow it. And I thought since you had your own apartment, with the spare room, maybe she could stay with you- I would pay you what I can, I wouldn't ask you to do it for free."

"G," Jecka interrupted, "We have never spoken of money being exchanged!"

"Come on Jecka, let me do this for you- what do you say Bryce? I think we'll all be happy if we let her stay with you, I said I would pay for her- huh?"

Bryce examined the situation for a moment. "Let's take a walk, er, roll for a minute- just you and me. Don't worry Jecka, we're not going to be talking about you- *much*." Bryce said as she rolled towards the door.

"Be right back." she nodded to Jecka as she walked out the door.

The two girls were traveling on the pathway to the cemetery when snow began to come down.

"This cemetery is beautiful, I've always thought." Bryce began.

"Me too."

"Why do you want me take her, really?"

"I still can never keep things from you, can I?" Gentry smiled.

"NO, you can't. Now spill- why this girl, why now?"

"Bryce, I didn't want to tell you because you're so anti-

72

religious. But I got her at the convent."

"The convent where you were born?"

"Uh- huh."

"Now it's getting good." Bryce's face lit up, "Why would you bring someone back from the convent to stay? Why were you at the convent at all? And for your information, I am *not* anti-religious! Where do you get these ridiculous ideas? Just because I'm not sure about how God works in this world- I'm ANTI-church, not anti-God."

"That's news to me! You certainly left the impression with me that you had become a true atheist. Anyway- the thing is- I went to the convent, and it was bad."

"Define bad."

"For one thing- the nun who so nasty to me died while I was there."

"That had to make you happy."

"I'm not sure. I'm confused. I wanted to ask her if I had a

73

sister- she would have been the only to ask since Sister Mary Alice had passed a few weeks ago."

"Whoa! Freeze right there- you have a sister? Shut up!" Bryce sat up in her chair and stopped, grasping Gentry's hands. She didn't believe G had a sister.

"Some things I found out while I was gone. Bryce, I still can't tell you where I was- so please don't even ask." her eyes were huge, staring down at Bryce.

Bryce's head turned down, it was obvious that she was hurt.

"I don't know how you can keep things from me- *me?*"

"If I could, I would- and I'll tell you all about it when it's finished- but I wouldn't put you into danger for anything! I promise! I'll tell you everything when I can." Gentry was trying to look in her eyes, but her head was turned away.

Suddenly, she turned her head around and said, "You'll tell me all! I want to know what secrets you've been keeping from me way back- back to the time I had my accident. I know that something happened to you that night- something fucking awful! You've never told me about that- and I want to know."

Gentry thought about that night- and the brutal rape that had occurred. She was right. She hadn't shared this secret with her- with anyone. That was the night the sky cracked open, and they had all been hit by shards of lightning.

"Tell me why you want me to hook her up, or is that part of your secret as well?"

"I took her from the convent because she asked. You should see the place, Bryce. It's god-awful- they have rats! They have no electricity...nothing. Most of the nuns seem to be imprisoned in that hole, and glad to do it! Jecka is different, she didn't want to be there. I couldn't be so mean as to make her stay."

"So it's me you've been saving your nastiness for?"

"Bryce! You don't mean that. The reason I want her to stay close is because I believe that she knows more than she's telling me about my sister-that is *if* she even exists!"

"I should tell you to go fuck yourself- that would be the right thing to do."

"Then I'd tell you to go to hell- oh wait- you're living there already!" Gentry spouted back, then regretted it.

"Why do I remain friends with you?" Bryce whispered.

"I honestly don't know. But I do love you, you know."

Bryce continued to roll further into the cemetery, towards the large angel statue. Even with the gray of the day it was beautiful in the graveyard, with the flurries gently covering the grave stones.

"I like this statue, the angel." Bryce whispered.

"I never knew that."

"She seems so strong. *So overpowering.* She's saying 'I make the living ride together with the dead.'"

Gentry walked up to the statue, and dusted off the snow.

"Jecka can stay with me. Don't forget her rent."

"Awww, Bryce. You're terrific. Thank you." she said as she put her arms around Bryce's neck and hugged her tight.

"Get off me, skank!"Bryce laughed. "Let's go get her." she said as she turned her wheelchair around and headed back for the house.

Chapter 7

Sitting at the university's library, Gentry was doing a background check on the ghost of Mrs. Manion's case. She would walk away shocked by what she learned at the end of the day.

She had checked at home, but her grandfather's history keeping was not as it's best as she was soon to discover. She found records, but she didn't find exactly what she needed to know. The prison had kept records together, but it was difficult to know who was who because they were kept by number, not by name. It was lucky for Gentry that the women were kept separate from men, that made it easier for her to ferret out. Gentry had found Mrs. M's burial certificate, but the information was sketchy at best. No family was listed in attendance, though it did say that the burial occurred in the dead of night, which made her curious. She decided to ask Jack if he remembered the

79

funeral, though she wasn't so sure he would even be on speaking terms with her. He was working in the embalming lab, as he was much of the time now.

"Dad?" she started.

"What is it, Gentry?" Jack said as he was cutting a body with a scalpel to put the embalming tube in the carotid.

"Could you answer a question for me?" she put on her best little girl voice which she hadn't used in years.

"Stop using that ridiculous tone of yours, and I might." he kept on working as he held the embalming tube in place with a forceps clamp.

"Sorry." she said, "I didn't mean to talk like a four year old, it's just that I do miss those days."

"Um hm." Jack was working on the eyes while the blood poured out of the veins while the embalming fluid took it's place. The eyes were important, Jack believed, the disks you placed under the eyelids made the person seem 'real',

80

gave them life.

"When you were a child, you watched your dad doing this job, right?"

"Yes. Seems like an eternity ago."

"Did your dad keep any records on the people he buried? I mean personal notes, not only the ones required by law?"

"I think he kept a personal diary, you know- how many people he would embalm in a week, notes about curiosities, physical oddities; I think he even had notes about the families that attended." Jack was still working on the left eye- it needed more cotton underneath the disk.

"REALLY? Do you think I could have a look?" Gentry was surprised as much as relieved.

"I don't know if it's even readable. It's in the attic, in a box. I think the cold may have got to that box. There!" now the eye's were perfect. Now for the lips, Jack was so good that he didn't even use glue to keep them together, he had a knack.

"Would you mind if I read it?"

"Now Gentry," Jack started, "why would you want to read a book like that?"

"I want to know grandpa better, I never even knew him. I also want to know as much as I can about the cemetery in the good ol days."

"Back then, when he started- I don't think they were legally required to keep records, other than who's buried where. I believe he even mentioned once that he had the contract for the prison. Of course, the prison has gone away. Too bad."

"There was a prison close by?"

"You know where that garbage refuse station is located? That's where the prison was situated. People didn't claim their bodies in those days- no sir! If a person was in prison and died- either by nature or execution, they stayed away,

Didn't claim 'em."

"Do you have records of people who came from the prison?" she was anxious now.

"Not just records, but that back couple acres we have, the one that looks grown over- we have the bodies buried there. If you push aside the weeds I believe you can still see some gravestones, of course they have numbers on them, not names."

"Really?" Gentry was elated. "So these records are grandpa's?"

"Yes."

"Same box as his diary? Are you sure you don't mind?"

"Gentry," Jack gravely said, "I hope you don't think we can do this forever."

"Do what?" she innocently asked.

"Go on pretending that the past didn't happen."

She looked away. She knew that they couldn't continue

either.

"Look dad," Gentry said, "I know I haven't been the most forthcoming- but there's a reason. Can you trust me with this until I get it figured out?"

"There's always a reason. Ella snarls at me because I can't get information out of you. There's a reason why I stay away from the house working all hours. There's a reason Katie walks like a god-damned zombie around the house. There's always a reason." Jack said as he dropped his scalpel onto the floor. "There's a reason I'm so fucking nervous that I dropped my scalpel!" Jack's voice was rising, she had never heard him talk like this.

"Dad, look- I'm sorry! But it's true- there's a reason I can't tell you! I promise to tell you soon, please?!" Gentry picked up his scalpel and handed it to him.

"Wash your hands. You're contaminated." as his voice returned to normal.

84

"Okay, I'll wash up right away." Gentry said as she was thinking, *I didn't know he kept a diary! I can't wait to find out what's in the friggin thing!*

Gentry had washed her hands and made her way onto the stairs that led to the attic. Once in the attic there was no heating, she shivered. There were boxes piled to the ceiling, with only a few of them marked. After three days of exhaustive searching she found the box with the diary, and the contract notes from the prison.

She gently went through the diary, as it was now tattered, torn and unreadable in some spots- all very intriguing. The notes on physical oddities were not politically correct, but he had them all. He had men whose bodies had been torn apart by war coming to meet their maker in crippled disguises. Men who didn't have legs or arms, there were men who had metal plates in their heads and even a man who didn't have a nose because it had been shot off in a bout of friendly fire.

Gentry almost fell over when she found a woman listed in the diary- *a woman named Matilda Manion!*

Gentry looked for further information on the woman, then gave it up for lost. *Screw it!*

Then to her surprise when she came across a super 8 projector. It was underneath some boxes that were molded and mildewed, and she wasn't even sure if it would work. She finally put it together, and was surprised when she plugged it in. It worked!

Fantastic! I can finally watch the films I picked up at the convent.

She ran downstairs to get the metal box and returned in a flash. Carefully she wound the delicate film around the projectors wheels and crossed her fingers. Gentry watched as a very young Mary Alice was the subject of the film. She looked *happy.* Where was she?

She wasn't in the convent, but outside. You could see in the background the charred outline of the barn, which had obviously been burnt to the ground. *There! In the corner- wasn't that the wisp of a ghost? No- It couldn't be a ghost.*

It was only on the screen for a second, but when Gentry backed the film to try and freeze- it broke! That was not going to stop her- she put a new roll of film onto the projector and started again. This scene was of a place she had never seen before. Dark and barely able to see through the shadows- she followed along with her breath held. It looked to be a school room of a girl who loved the romantic tales- they had all the books in place- *Pride & Prejudice, Jane Eyre, Wuthering heights and funny, a copy of Sherlock Holmes, along with the Holy Bible. And that couldn't be- yet it was, a copy of The Poems of Emily Dickenson! THE POEMS OF EMILY DICKENSON!! The very poet whose poems went in and out of my mind.*

The film ran out, and Gentry put in another roll of film- but it was only the nuns in their sitting room- all much younger, of course. But, the person who was filming, the document-or was never shown- it had to be Catherine. Why else would she have these films underneath her bed? Where was that film taken- it had to be close by- if not *in* the convent itself. The film where she had seen a ghost was out in back of the convent- she was sure of that- but why would Catherine want documentation of a ghost? Was it to prove to Father Adams that they indeed *did* have a ghost? Perhaps they wanted documentation to have proof that they needed some sort of blessing on the place- like an exorcism.

Why Catherine, why? I'm getting tired of having more questions pop up every time I think I'm getting closer!

Gentry went to the library the next day, determined to find answers. She pulled out genealogies of people named

Manion who had died in the area of upper Washington. They would have had to die sometime between 1840 and 1960- a long time. Her eyes were getting tired after an afternoon of looking and she stopped and rubbed her red eyes. She continued into the evening.

Suddenly she came across two boys, ages 8 and 12 who died simultaneously, and further down the page she found their father who died the same day. They didn't die of Spanish flu- but instead were murdered simultaneously! The entry did not mention anything about their mother or who did the killing- Gentry was befuddled.

If this is the correct family, then why does it say they were murdered? Where's the mention of Spanish flu? Could it be Mrs. M had not been honest with her? How did these boys die, is that why Mrs. M was in prison?

Back to the books, she was set to stay there until the library closed, which was midnight? She checked with the librarian to be sure, then she went to look in her books once more.

Gentry scoured the library until she found the books she needed, including an old pamphlet that had a multitude of information. The pamphlet followed the old prison from the days when it opened in 1866 to the final days in 1966.

The prison had started out as a pig farm, but not a successful one, and was turned into a prison in 1866- so it was a prison for approximately 100 years total.

On the first pages the pamphlet followed the beginnings of the prison, where they put prisoners from shoplifting to the section where they held the most gruesome murderers. Now it getting interesting.

One of the most infamous was the section where the prison had it's first woman convicted of murder-*a triple murder!* Gentry perked up when she found the name of the woman hanged was Matilda Manion. Gentry read further

90

and found that Matilda had concocted this atrocity by putting arsenic into the boys daily soup. Her neighbors all gave her great sympathy and the doctor's were all stumped. Her husband was starting to get suspicious and demanded to know what was happening. She denied it all and the boys seemed to get better, as she stopped using the arsenic, her husband was close to finding her out. Until one night- the night when all hell broke loose. When the boys and their father had gone to bed, they did not know that she had put herbs such as Valerian, and chamomile into their nightly drink; she wanted to make sure they would be drowsy for what happened next.

First she attacked her husband hitting him squarely in the back of the head with an ax. It was estimated at her trial that she hit him no less than 15 times- more than enough to kill- it was an act of rage. Then, she went into the boys room- and again her rage showed when she hit each boy more than 10 times each in the head, breaking the handle of the ax while she was murdering the last boy. Matilda thought she could get away with the act of carnage by pretending that she had slept through the killings, but the police saw through the lie immediately. So did Gentry, she recognized Munchhausen's syndrome, even if it had occurred so long ago.

She was jailed, convicted and sentenced to hang. The fact that she was a woman and this her whole family was difficult for the jury to process, but they had done their duty when she was convicted of murder in the first degree on all three counts. They had said that mental instability was the reason she had snapped, Gentry knew better. *I guess having Munchhausen's at any time should get you convicted, even if it was unrecognizable back then.*

Matilda was the first and only woman to face the death penalty in the life of the prison.

92

This must be Mrs. M, she lied to me! She has to know what she did, but why would she want to know where her family lay? She can't want to hurt them again, would she? What could she do- she was a ghost, after all.

Gentry put the pamphlet back on the reading rooms table. This was *not* what she had hoped to find. She let out a big sigh, but it was intriguing stuff.

Chapter 8

On a day when snowed and turned to slush, Gentry was out on her turn to oversee the funeral processions of a young child, a boy of 3 and a half years. There was some weeping and his parents were clinging to each other, they seemed to be cried out. The priest was a common part of the procession, as most people didn't have a priest that they professed was their own she often called Father Alex.

Father Alex was 65 years old and had retired the year before, but was always on call when people needed a priest for funerals. Gentry was well acquainted with Father Alex, but she never spoke to him about anything but funerals, and the loved ones left behind.

Father Alex was coming to the end of his well practiced speech about how deeply the departed had touched our lives, and then on to the prayer. Gentry knew her line and got up in front of the chapel to tell the crowd that they

would proceed to the spot in the graveyard and have a
final prayer as they lowed the coffin. She cued the men
who were going to lift the small coffin to the hearse, then
drove about 100 yards to the area of the cemetery known
as 'Little Angels', an area that they only buried children.
Father Alex proceeded to the head of the casket and
started to say a prayer in Latin, which people chimed in
with the appropriate refrains.

When the last prayer was finished, and the last person
had left, Gentry walked over to Father Alex. He spoke,
"How is the hardest working mortician today?"
Gentry laughed to herself. She never thought of what she
did as work. "I'm fine, Father Alex. How about you?"
Father Alex smiled wearily, he looked like he was
ancient, but dedicated as ever. "Fine, I suppose. The
arthritis is acting up- but I'll get by."

"Don't you ever think of retiring, I mean from this." she

96

said as her hand turned towards the cemetery.

"Retiring? From this? *Nooooo*. This isn't working so much- I feel as though I have a responsibility to the children in my flock. I'm escorting them to the hereafter."

"I believe I know what you mean, Father. I feel a responsibility as well. Someone has to make people palatable to be seen after death comes. But you know what?"

"What is that, child?"

"It always hits me when I think of the person we just buried, about the mother and father. They were used to being parents- getting food ready for him to eat, taking him to the park to play- suddenly, they are not there anymore to be taken care of. Parents one day and 'boom' next day it's taken away from them. I find that terribly sad."

"Yes. I never think of the people left behind- I suppose

97

because it's my job to get their souls up to heaven."

Suddenly, he froze, his eyes were looking over Gentry's shoulder. She turned to look, but did not see a thing. She turned back and tried to look into Father Alex's deeply hooded eyes- but he would not respond.

"Father Alex, what's wrong?"

"I don't know. I must be getting too old for this." he waved his hand over the graveyard.

Gentry was immediately curious, as she looked around to see if she could see what was in his vision

"I think I saw...no, no."

"Go ahead, Father- what did you see?"

"Saints Almighty! I think I saw a ghost!" he said as the blood drained away from his elderly face.

"Where? What did you see- specifically?"

"I know it must be a hallucination. I know I couldn't have seen a ghost. But it looked like a woman, a little old lady- dressed in white and floating right there!" he pointed across the cemetery to the largest Angel statue in the cemetery, where she had first met Mrs. M- and the description fit her to a T.

"Father, I'm going to take you inside. You're chilly and tired. You're seeing things." Gentry walked up next to him and grabbed him by the arm and gently led him inside. "Let's get you some tea, and out of this weather."

"But I could have sworn- saints be gone, it looked like a lady in white- I must be mad!" he covered his eyes with his hands, then blinked several times.

The blood slowly returned to the priests face as he drank the tea Gentry brought. "You won't tell what I saw, will you?"

"No, Father. I won't tell."

She finally got the Father to leave when he seemed like himself again.. Then she stood at the porch bundled in her black, funeral coat and watched him drive away.

WTF? I will be talking to Mrs. Manion tonight, no doubt.

The moon was bright that night, although at times it would hide behind clouds. She put on her warmest black winter coat and gloves and started to walk over to the far side of the cemetery first- to where the little boys bodies were hidden. She had never *seen* them before- she had only heard about them from Mrs. M. Secretly, she had previously dug up two pairs of hands to obtain DNA from the children, but it was too terrible to see them whole- and the DNA *was* a match to the evil man.

Her footing made an audible 'crunch' just as she saw the outline of the boys ghosts. They turned to Gentry and huddled together as if they were afraid.

"Please don't go. I want to talk to you....just talk...okay?" She saw them whisper in each others ears, they turned as if they wanted to disappear.

100

"I won't hurt you...I promise. Stay and talk to me."

Just then one of the boys turned again, and disappeared 'whoosh', right into the wall. There was only one boy left, and he was kicking the dirt in front of him.

"You want to talk?" he asked in his most grown up voice.

"Yes, please."

"What about?"

"How you got here. Can you tell me about how you got here, I mean I know who the man is- I think. But I need to hear it from you."

"You *know* the scary man?" he turned as if he wanted to disappear, and she unsure how to make him stay.

"I have met the scary man, he wanted to hurt me too."

"But you got away?"

"Yes. I did. Barely."

"I didn't." he said as he looked at Gentry as if she had the answer to questions unknown.

101

"Did he have another scary man bury you here?"

"How do you know that?" he said now talking with his little boy voice.

"I know because I have met the scary man, and his helpers." Slowly the other little boys appeared, but stayed back.

There was no answer from the boy, but she could sense that there was a circle of trust between the boys, and she had now broken it with talk. They knew much more than talk- they knew what the evil man could, and would do. Gentry tried again. "Would you do me a favor?"

"Depends."

"Do you think you could get the other boys together so we all could talk together, hmmm?" she got down on her knees to level out the playing field.

"Come back tomorrow." he said using the authority he held over Gentry.

"Okay. I'll come back this time, tomorrow." she got up off her knees and slowly backed away, and suddenly he was gone.

She headed towards the angel statue, where Father Alex had seen the ghost that day, and she was screaming mad. The crispness of the snow crunched under her feet and it was the noise that Mrs. M heard as she turned around and greeted Gentry. Mrs. M looked weary, as weary as a ghost can look and her welcome was strange.

"You look how I feel." Mrs. Manion said in her weakened voice.

"I have to talk to you." she announced.

"About what, my young child?"

"Don't even try to talk nice to me- you let Father Alex see you today! Why on earth would you try to scare an old man like that?" her voice sounded like her blood was hot.

"Old man? HMMPFF! What do I care about an old

man?" Mrs. Manion tried to equal Gentry's rage.

"Don't you have feelings for anyone but yourself?"

"Oh, don't be mad at me- besides, that 's not why you came here anyway."

"You're right- he's not." Mrs. Manion started floating back and forth. It made Gentry dizzy.

"Keep still- so we can talk."

Mrs. Manion slowly stopped. Gentry continued.

"Why didn't you tell me that you died a prisoner?"

"It did not matter to what we talked about."

"So, it was you! I couldn't be sure till I asked you. Of course it matters, if you wanted to try and trick me..."

"Why would I do that?" she said in a curious way. "Did you find out why I was imprisoned?" she asked quickly.

"Yes. Since that lady I read about was you-your a murderer! You murdered your whole family."

"I do not remember doing that! I remember being in

debtor's prison. That's it. Now you promised to try to find my boys, and my husband- you must!" Mrs. Manions voice grew louder.

"Look here, Mrs. M," Gentry was confused. She seemed to be such a *nice* old lady, but... "something fishy is going on here. I don't know what it is, but this isn't right."

"You do what you promised me, that's what you'll do. And you better deliver!" she said sternly.

"I will keep looking for them, because I promised. But if I feel I've been lied to or mislead I'll..I'll...." Gentry stopped for a moment. What could she do? "I'll stop immediately!"

"What could be wrong with a wife and mother trying to find her loved ones' after death? What could be more natural?" then her tone changed and she became bigger than before. "Remember, you can't shield them forever, so if you want to protect your little boys here," she pointed to

105

the shallow graves with a bony finger, "I would get busy figuring out where *my* family is buried."

"I knew it wasn't right! If you so much as sneeze towards those boys, I'll...I'll..." Gentry was stumped, she didn't know what she *would* do; but she knew it might come down to stopping Mrs. Manion.

"You'll do what? I sounds to me like I have you cornered!" she started to laugh. Gentry was at an impasse. She would have to get the boys to help- but she couldn't talk to them till tomorrow. She started to walk away. She heard a faint mumbling, "You promised! You have made a serious mistake if you think you can try and fool me."

Gentry looked back, but her ghost was gone. A chill went down her spine.

....

Gentry walked back through the cemetery, crunching the snow that had turned to ice. Her thoughts were heavy as she reached the back porch, took off her galoshes then made her way back inside. She hadn't noticed that Katie was standing there, looking at her, standing still as a statue. Gentry was startled.

"Katie!" she said her voice filled with surprise, "What are you doing there? Are you spying on me?"

"I was watching you." Katie sounded like she was in a trance once more.

"And?"

"Why do you talk when there's no one there? I saw you just a minute ago, talking to the air right behind that angel statue."

"You don't know what you're talking about, Katie. Go to bed."

"Why does everyone want me to go to bed? Mom says go to bed, the doctors say go to bed- I don't want to dream, Gentry. My dreams are vile, they're absolutely ghastly!

107

They keep me on these wretched pills that make me sleep- they make me *dream.* " Katie said with a bit of coherency.

She sounded more like Katie, and less like a zombie.

"Do you want to talk, I mean, do you want to talk to me?" Gentry said with a bit of surprise, both to her asking and to Katie's nodding her head.

"I would-yes."

Gentry took her by the arm and led her back to her bedroom- such a thing never happened before.

. . . .

The following night it was sure that there would be a full moon *if* the sky remained cloudless; but the sky had spotty patches all afternoon. Gentry tiptoed into the graveyard from a different direction so she might avoid seeing Mrs. Manion and meet the boys. It was colder that night, and the snow had been falling all day, it had finally stopped when Gentry walked back for their meeting. Yes! The three boys were there, waiting for her to arrive.

"Hello. Your friend here said I would be able to meet you all- and here you are. I'm so grateful you have decided to meet with me."

"We were all wondering what it is that you want from us?" the boy from last night did their talking for them.

"Am I that transparent?"

The boys all went into a huddle, whispering then asked, "What does trans-prnt mean?"

"I'm sorry. I just meant...nothing." she realized that she was going to have to use small words. "Are you boys cold out here?"

"No. We're fine. Nothing bothers us." the little boys said.

"Oh. Because we have a huge tool shed that you're more than welcome to use." The boys huddled again then asked her, "We figure that's not what you wanted to meet us for."

109

"You're right- you're all right, there." she was nervous, shifting from one foot to another. She was going to have to come out with it. "What are your names? I believe I have heard them, but I would like to know who I am talking with- on a more personal level."

The little boy who was talking to her first said, "My name is Finn. This one, his name is Broderick and finally that one is called Randy. What is your name?"

"My name is Gentry. Nice to meet you." she said as she got down on her knees to talk. They seemed to be pleased with her action and came closer.

"What I wanted to talk to you about is this-why do you boys stay? I mean, why didn't your spirits go to heaven?" she asked them with all sincerity, not wanting to have them leave for asking a stupid question. Finn it seems, was talking for all three when he said, "We couldn't. I mean we would love it if we could go- someplace other than here.

110

But our spirits are tied to our bodies, at least until they, our parents, find us and have us moved."

"That's what I thought. And do you know that I am searching for the evil man who sent you here?"

"No. We thought we were forgotten by now."

Gentry's thoughts turned to anger at the evil man, and for his sending children to a wicked eternity such as this. They also turned to guilt at herself for not telling the authorities that they were here, that she had found them and was keeping it to herself. Luckily, that didn't seem to be a problem with the boys.

"No. You're not forgotten at all. I want to promise you, all of you, that I will find him, and I will destroy him!" she said trying to keep her voice down. A small cheer went up for her from the boys, and Finn spoke again, "Thank you, so much! If there's anything we can ever do for you- we will do it."

111

"That's good. I think there will be something you can do."

"Name it."

"I need you to tell me- is there a way I can trap a person, a ghost, such as yourselves?" she was finally getting excited.

"A trap? Oh yes, there's a lot of traps! We play around them all the time."

Gentry pulled herself closer to the boys so they could talk in whispers. This is what she needed, helpers who were willing to trap Mrs. Manion.

…..

There was a sudden shift in the cold breeze, a change that came with the name of Alfie. Alfie stepped out a small statue with a cherub on top. He was about 14 years old, young enough to be buried in the children 's section but he felt so much older, and as such he crowned himself King of the young angels, and he wore a phony crown on his head, but believed it was real.

"You there, what are you doing with these boys?" he announced.

Gentry was a little startled by his sudden presence, but she quickly figured out who he was, and thought that she had better get on his good side. She stood up straight and made a bow to Alfie. When she gave him respect, it surprised him and he bowed back, nearly knocking his crown to the ground- but he reached out and caught it neatly.

"I see that your name is Alfred, sir."

"Most people call me Alfie- you can call me *Sir Alfie.*"

"I know that you saw me talking to the boys; perhaps you would like to help us? It's for a wonderful cause I can assure you."

"What is this 'cause' you speak of?"

113

"Well you see," Gentry started slowly, she had to be sure to put this in the best light possible. "These boys were buried here by a monster of a man."

"Yes. I remember a skinny man digging their graves." he said as he stroked where his beard would be, if he had been old enough to have one.

"That man *was* skinny, but NO! The man who buried them here wasn't the monster, though he was vile. There was another evil man, a ghoulish man who killed these boys and had them buried here all the while leaving their parents to wonder if they would get them back- which they wouldn't- not alive, at least."

"What? *NO!* Why have you boys never told me this?" he sounded like a big brother, so Finn spoke.

"It was a secret! We had made a pact with each other *never* to tell how we got here. She seemed to know already!" He pointed at Gentry.

114

"Yes," she hurriedly spoke, "I know about the man who was responsible- and I will get him for doing what he did. But I need their help, and I suppose I need your help as well, Sir Alfie!"

"What do you mean, you need our help?" Alfie's voice cracked, he unfortunately died in the middle of puberty.

"I need help in getting one of your ghosts in a trap somehow. I need to get rid of her before she does a terrible deed to her dead husband and children."

"Terrible deed?"

"Yes. I don't know what she is planning exactly- but I do know it is evil. She killed them, her husband and two boys while she lived. She is seeking them now in death and I can't let her find them- I simply can't!" Gentry was trying to steady her voice, but she was shaking. "The boys were telling me about a trap I could use?"

"Well, how about it boys? Do you know a trap that is

115

unknown to me?" Sir Alfie sounded like he wanted to help, but he was unsure of a trap. Surely there would be no trap that he didn't know of.

Bryan whispered in Finn's ear, then Finn squared his shoulders and said, "We play with traps all the time, you were too busy to notice."

"That can't be. I pay attention to every little thing that happens in my area of the cemetery!"

"That's why you never noticed- because you ONLY pay attention to what happens here- in this area. There are plenty of parts where we wander off into- you wouldn't even think of looking for us in other parts of the cemetery." Finn said proudly.

Sir Alfie looked deflated. He had been sure that there wasn't a place in the whole cemetery where he didn't make sure to check-but had he really? He straightened out his crown once again and continued to stroke his invisible beard, he looked like he was deep in thought as he wandered around his gravestone. He looked at Finn and said, "You there, yes- you!"

Finn glared back at Alfie and said, "Yes? Don't you believe us?"

"I gave what you told me and I considered: that -yes- there might be a place or two where I have NOT wandered across. Show us, please, where are these *traps?*"

Finn looked at Broderick and Randy, he shrugged his shoulders. "Come on, they're over here."

Anxiously they all walked over past a huge stone family mausoleum surrounded by pine trees on both sides. The name 'Suson' was etched in grey stone above the locked door, but they were able to float right through the bars. The boys continued to walk past the large sarcophagi with all but Gentry following. She got out the keys she had for the cemetery, hoping that the key to this particular

117

mausoleum were on her set. After a few tries, she found the right key and walked in after the group.

Sir Alfie looked around the tomb and said, "Well? Where is this trap? I don't see a thing."

"Watch this!" Finn giggled as he dropped an old leaf he had found, down near the head of the sarcophagus. There was a 'whoosh' sound and the leaf disappeared. They all stared in disbelief!

"Where did it go?" Alfie was astounded.

"I'm not sure- but I *did* make it disappear, didn't I?" The three boys all laughed and then put their heads together and whispered again.

"And you say that this is one of your traps? That means that you've found another." Gentry anxiously gasped.

"WE have found another-yes."

"Then tell me where this other suck hole exists! I demand to know." Sir Alfie said.

118

"You have to know the password!" Randy suddenly shouted, "Give us the password!"

"*Me?*" Sir Alfie questioned. "I don't need to *know* the password! I DEMAND to know where this other trap is located!"

Randy stuck his tongue out at Sir Alfie, being very obstinate. Alfie grew red and he was angry, he grabbed Randy by the arm and pulled him up to where they were face to face.

"Listen, you...I have total authority in our area of the cemetery...you don't want me as an enemy!"

Gentry had enough. "That's it!" she shouted, "Let him go Sir Alfie!"

Alfie reluctantly let the squirming boy down on the ground.

"We have to stick together! There are monsters out there- and the only way we can overcome them is to stay tight-together! We have to be able to trust each other- and that means we need to be mature about it."

Alfie looked down at his feet, starting to squirm.

"You're right. I'm sorry young man, please accept my apology." Alfie said as he put his hand out to Randy.

Randy stopped backing away, the boys Broderick and Finn circled around him.

"Alright," Randy began, "I accept your apology." he put his hand out for a friendly handshake.

"But you better not do it again!" Finn said suddenly.

"I won't, little man- you have my word." Sir Alfie said as he crossed his heart.

Gentry was glad when the apologies were behind them, now, they could continue. "Tell us, show us where the other trap is located!"

Finn pointed with his finger to the edge of the cemetery. There was a small bush, in this part of the graveyard,

120

small, dead and thorny. The group walked up to the bush and watched while Finn picked up a branch, then dropped it behind-it went with another 'whoosh' before it too was gone.

"This is fantastic!" Gentry said, "And you say you have no idea of where it leads?"

"No. None at all." Finn answered, giggling all the while.

"These are dangerous, you know." Sir Alfie said, "You don't know where they go, but you play around them. How do you know they won't suck you up while you're playing around them?"

"I don't know where they go, but I doubt they could be worse than being dead and stuck in this cemetery!" Finn started to tear up, he didn't want them to see him cry, he didn't want them to think he was a baby. He turned away from the group.

"Sir Alfie is right, though. Since you don't know where

121

they go, you should stay away from them. I mean, perhaps this is a portal straight to hell." Gentry tried to sound as authoritative as she could. But she didn't have a clue. This was a question for the grim reaper, perhaps he knew. She knew one thing though, she was definitely going to put one of these traps to good use.

Chapter 9

The following day Gentry was up to her neck in maps and building permits at the city hall for the convent. She now knew the layout for the pipes and heating vents, she knew that the building, or at least most of it, was constructed in 1907. She found the permit for the barn, which was added much later in 1945. She found that the property was owned by an old childless couple until they both passed away leaving the property to the church in 1947. She also saw that the only name she could find, besides the old couples name was that of a lawyer, who had overseen the transfer- Levi Addison, jr.

Long dead, no doubt. But I'll write that name down and look him up.

Then she saw what she did not expect- Tunnels! Tunnels running through the convent and to the barn.

Tunnels! That's it! They have tunnels running through

the heart of the convent!

She ran to the copier with arms loaded down with originals of the maps. Furiously she made copies for her to take home and study.

I wonder if Jecka knew about the tunnels? She shouldn't have knowledge of them, no one would unless they were the ones to use them, or knew where to look for them in the first place. I'll bet those tunnels were known to Catherine and Mary Alice- they had to know all!

Gentry ran out of the library with her copies under her arms, then stuffed them into her backpack before she got on her motorcycle and headed for home. Of course that made sense, that means that in the tunnels was where they would have had to keep her sister, a place where no one else knew about, a place that they could have privacy from the other nuns, that is until they got another couple to adopt her- there had to be paperwork of some kind to tell

124

her about a possible adoption for her sister. Jecka had to know where such paperwork was kept- anything.

As soon as she got home she went to her computer- it was time to look up this attorney. There was a Levi Addison listed, but it was Levi Addison, III.

He must have died or retired, but his son should have access to his files! Quickly she wrote down his number and address, which was here in town, just blocks away. She tried to call, but repeatedly got no answer, only an answering machine.

Gentry decided to go see Mr. Addison and find out what happened. She knocked on his door, but it looked like he was out of business. The door was taped up and the windows were boarded as well. There was a small notice in one of the windows, 'For Lease, by owner.' and it had a phone number! She dialed this number into her phone and after it rang 10 times, a man answered.

125

"Hello?" he said.

She decided to sound like she was a perspective leaser, she figured this would be the quickest way.

"Hello? My name is Gentry. I'm interested in leasing your building?"

"When do you want to see the property?" he mumbled. She could tell he had a hangover.

"Right away. I'm at the property right now, actually."

"Huh,..." you could hear the desperation in his voice, but then he said, "Okay. I'll be right there."

"I'll be right here." Gentry was psyched. She sat at a coffee shop across the street and waited there for him to arrive. She was sipping the last of her cocoa when he pulled up in a rattly, old Toyota. She immediately got up and walked towards him.

"Mr. Addison?"

"You know my name? Why? Who are you?" he was

126

suspicious right off.

"Mr. Addison, my name is Gentry, I told you that over the phone already. I wanted to talk to you about a deal your father was involved in."

"Then call me Levi, *Mr.* Addison was my father. I don't have money if you've come to collect any debts."

"Take it easy, old man! I just want to ask you a few questions about your father's business- that's all."

"Buy me a cup of joe, then perhaps I'll talk." he eased, and she was anxious.

"Okay. Come on." They walked across the street and she bought him a large cup of coffee when he said, "And put a couple of rolls into a bag. That's right, I'll take those."

She realized that he was broke. They sat down in the tables they had on the sidewalk, grateful customers were happy because he smelled like he hadn't taken a bath in a week. As he chowed down on the rolls and gulped his

127

coffee he said, "Now, what do you want to know? I have the key to that building, that was all ours. Now, it's gone."

"What do mean? Did you spend the money your dad left you?" she asked.

"Yeah. I did. Wine, women and song, ya know? They don't come easy, or cheap." he wiped his mouth with his tattered old sleeve.

"I wanted to find out about this deal he made with an old childless couple, to leave their land to the church? Do you know what case I'm talking about?"

"Oh, yeah. I remember that case. He made a lot of money off that couple. Wills, transfers- they all cost money, ya know? I remember him laughing at the couple."he snorted.

"Be that the case," she started, "I wanted to know the specifics, like *who* was it that oversaw the transfer to the church? I mean, I know your father did, but *who* was the person, not the church, who actually signed the

128

paperwork?" her eyes told him how desperate she was to find out.

"I think that this is going to worth a *whole lot more, than* a couple of rolls." his eyes turned to narrow slits.

Chapter 10

Gentry knew that he was going to be a hard sell. She wanted information, that only he had. Now she feared she was going to have to give this awful man whatever he wanted to get it. Or *scare* him into giving away the information. She figured that if she was scared of the evil man, that he would be too.

"You say you have the information I'm asking for," she slowly started.

"Yes. I do."

"Was this man, who overtook the property- was he frightening to you as he was to me?" she asked with a grin.

"You mean...you don't mean...he's still alive?" he stuttered. Suddenly he started to sweat.

"Yes. He's alive. He's living only miles from here. Here, I can give you his number, if you want." she toyed with him.

"But I thought that surely, he'd be dead, *yes dead* by now. He was so old then, so terribly old. That was maybe 60 years ago, I was but a child!" a small trail of goo was on his chin, it turned Gentry's stomach to look at him.

"So, I'm assuming that it was *that* man who took possession of the property?.."

"Yes, yes...it was him. NO! Don't give him my number, please, *please.*" he begged.

"I promise, I won't- *if* you tell me what this charm means." she pulled out the charm she had since she first found out about her father and handed it to him. He took it at first, curious. Then he dropped it as if it burned his fingers and said, "No! I haven't the fainted idea of what that is!"

"Listen! You tell me now, old man- what this charm means to you- or I will personally escort the man to your

132

door! Tell me what it means!" her hands grabbed him by the torn jacket that he wore.

"Okay. Okay. I'll tell you- but then you have to swear that you won't tell *him*. Do we have a deal?"

"Okay."

"That charm is from Romania. There's some writing on the back, it's Romanian. It *was* his. He would wear it around his neck with a gold chain."

"Is that where's he's from, Romania? Is that where his home is?" she snapped.

"I think so. Master Herman would speak other languages, other times in English. But I've only seen him once, and as I said before, I was but a small child."

"You called him 'Master Herman- is that his name?"

"I've told you too much! Forget that I mentioned his name- *please.*" he was crying and slobbering.

"Okay, okay. I'll forget it. I'll forget everything we've

talked about. IF, you go about your business and forget that I was ever here. Do we have a deal?"

"Yes, yes...thank you. Yes, forget....forget."

Gentry threw a ten dollar bill on the table which he was meant to get as a gesture of good will. But instead he ran toward his car without looking either way, crying still. She thought she saw a shadow out of the corner of her eye. She turned to see it was the grim reaper, laughing as usual. Then a passing bus hit Levi square on the chest as he was blubbering when it hit, and threw him 100 yards. The bus screeched to a stop; his body lay there torn and broken, he moved no more. She stood there and looked at where he stood just 2 seconds ago. Then she saw the ten dollar bill dancing in circles, blown away by the wind. The grim reaper took a bow, smiled, then turned his cloak and left.

Chapter 11

Gentry bypassed the road to her home and sped away towards Bryce's house.

She pulled up to the house and was downright chilled, but she kept her head on the mystery that had to be solved. She knocked furiously on the door until finally Jecka answered the door.

"Jecka," she began, "I need to ask you some questions about the convent- serious questions!"

"Gentry," Jecka said in her soft voice, "Please come in and warm yourself- you look cold."

"I am cold but,God damn it! I don't want to warm up- I want answers! Hopefully you can give me that." Gentry grabbed her by the shoulders. Bryce came rolling into the room.

"Gentry- hey, what are doing with her?"

"Bryce, I need to ask Jecka some questions about the

135

convent- and I don't have time to shield you from answers today. Pretend you're deaf and leave us alone."

"Like hell I will!" Bryce demanded, "I'm finally going to hear about you and this bloody convent-go on, I'm listening."

Gentry stomped her foot on the floor. She did *not* want to go into this in front of Bryce. She had no other choice.

"Bryce!" she yelled, then continued, "Okay. But I reserve the right not to explain."

The wind came whipping into the room, Jecka closed the door and shivered. "What is it? What do you want to know?"

"I want you to tell me about the tunnels running beneath the convent. I want you to tell me where those wicked nuns would have kept paperwork on another adoption- the adoption for my *older sister!*"

Jecka's face went white. She had to sit down. She said,

"Your older sister?!"

Bryce continued with her voice betraying her skepticism, "You're not going to go back to that are you? How do you even know you have a sister?"

Gentry sighed deeply, "I know I was born the youngest of triplets, with a brother and sister born before me. This I know! Jecka, You must know where papers are kept- my adoption papers?"

Jecka's mouth had dropped open. Gentry grabbed her by the shoulders once again.

"How would I know about that?" Jecka finally managed to get out. "The sisters *never* showed me papers on an adoption."

"Never? Not even once?"

"No, nev-" She stopped mid-sentence. She had put her hand to her forehead. "OH MY GOD! I do know where they put *my* papers when I first came to live there they

137

filled out some paperwork on me, and then put it in a

file box- a *secret* file box! But it was locked- so if they do

have paperwork I have no idea about where the key would

be."

"I do." Gentry raised the key from around her neck that

she had taken from around Catherine's neck. Now Gentry

knew where the mysterious key led.

138

<u>Chapter 12</u>

Gentry grasped the key in her hand and shouted, "Let's go!"

"Wait up!" Bryce raced towards them, "I want to go with you."

"Bryce, I don't have a way to take you."

"We'll use my van."

"But once we get there, there's not a ramp at the convent. I couldn't get you inside."

"They have to have a ramp, it's the law..." Bryce argued.

"They're the church. They don't have to follow the law. Besides, it's an old decrepit building- the floors are falling apart in places- I couldn't live with myself if I let anything happen to you." Gentry was still trying to get Bryce to stay- as much as she cared for Bryce, the last thing she needed was another person to protect.

139

"There's two of you- you can lift me up the stairs to the entry. Now, let's get the fuck out of here!" There was no way Bryce was going to be left behind on a deal this important. Besides, she hadn't had anything exciting happen to her since the accident, and this was exhilarating!

"Okay, okay. Let's go." Gentry gave in with a sigh.

"Wait!" Jecka suddenly shouted.

"What?" Bryce asked.

"I do not want to go back there. What if they make me stay? I am serious, I am scared." Jecka was trembling.

"I don't think that's going to happen- but you're right." Gentry thought for a moment, "We can sneak in there at night, after the nuns are sleeping- they sleep on the second floor, right?"

Jecka nodded her head.

"Then we'll wait till later, when it's darker-what time did

140

you go to bed?"

"8 or 9, depending on what time of year it was."

"Till then, you can tell me about the tunnels."

Bryce was so excited her hands were shaking. "What tunnels are you talking about, G?"

"I was at the city hall earlier- I came across these." she got her backpack off and pulled out the copies of the tunnels. She un-crumpled them on the table. "See? There's tunnels all over the place, you just have to know where to look."

"I have never seen them, honest I have not!" Jecka's voice was shaky.

"So, in all the time you were there-5 years, wasn't it-you've never seen another person use the tunnel system, ever?"

"No, never."

"I have to believe that at least two of the nuns knew about

141

them- I think it was Catherine and Mary Alice."

"They may have, but honestly- I have never even heard about them."

"We'll have a look when we arrive tonight. Is that alright with you, Jecka?"

"I am still scared, but yes, if you want to go back there tonight, I will go. You have all been so kind to me, I did not know people could be so kind- I will do whatever I can to help you." Jecka put her fist outward.

"Remember Gentry? You taught me this."

Gentry and Bryce put their fists on a bump with Jecka's.

"Hey," Bryce was giddy, "We're like the 3 Musketeers, all over again!"

Gentry had a bad feeling come over her like a wave when she said this- it reminded her of the last time the 3 Musketeers was mentioned- on the night of the accident and her rape. She forced herself to say, "Yes, we are."

142

Gentry suddenly remembered what day of the week it was- Saturday!

"I promised to be in Seattle tonight. I have to leave for a few hours- I'll be back tonight- I promise."

"Where do you think you're off to?" Bryce asked with a twinkle in her eyes.

"I promised Q that I would meet him at the docks."

Bryce let out a small whelping noise. "Who is this Q? What does he have to do with all this? Answer me truthfully girl, I can tell when you're lying to me."

"Q is a guy I met when I was getting Katie back- I didn't mention him to you because he's trouble, I guess. I needed his kind of trouble to get Katie back."

"Then why are you going to see him now? You don't need to get Katie back- she's home."

"We're friends, that's all. I have a few things I needed to get straight about that night."

143

"Oh, you fucking liar!" Bryce laughed, "Go ahead and go. I'll get the truth out of you when you get back."

"Whatever! I'll see you in a few hours." Gentry said as she walked out the door.

God, she's fucking nosy...but I'm glad to have her on my side.

....

Gentry finally sped into Seattle where she parked her bike near the Pier 55 that she had agreed to meet Q. She looked around and did not see him immediately, so she walked over to the fast food line that had wonderful smells wafting over. When it was her turn to order, Q jumped in line with her, ordered and paid for the entire amount.

"Why would you do that, Q? I have money."

"If you don't want it- which I think you do- you can throw it in the ocean when the guy brings it over."

144

They walked over to the bench that was least occupied, and sat down.

"No. I won't do that. Thanks." she said as the waiter brought her steamy fish. Q had an order of octopus. He loaded it with hot sauce and dug right in.

"So, what is it you want from me?" Q asked with suspicion in his voice.

"I already told you, I don't *want* things from you." She threw her legs over the bench and whispered, "Look, I have questions that only you can answer."

"And what do I get in return?" he said making his eyebrows go up and down.

"Look Q- I...."

"Crips! I'm kidding." he took a long laugh at her, she was so serious. "Look, I was trying to get you to laugh. You've got to be less tense."

She relaxed.

"You have questions for me, right?" he said as he kicked her boot under the table.

"Yes." she said as she pulled her leg back as far as it would go.

"For instance?" he paused. "What do you want to drink?" he asked.

"Anything of the Pibb variety."

He got up from the table and went over to the drink bar and got them the drinks. The waiter had brought potato skins over to their table-steamy and perfect!

"Continue."

"I had already known that you survive as a smuggler...now wait- I don't care about what you're smuggling or for who." she said.

He looked over his shoulder, as if he were making sure they weren't being watched. He gave her a curious look.

"What is it you want? Money?" he whispered in a tone

that was almost inaudible.

Her face soured and she twisted her lips. "No! That's *not* what I want." she turned to stand and he grabbed her by the hand, but his grasp was so gentle it caught her off guard. She sat back down and gazed at Q.

"What I want- the whole reason I came here- I need to know about that castle. I know you've been back there- am I right?"

Q didn't know what to do, or say. But he didn't want to lie to Gentry after all they've gone through.

"Yes."

"They're gone now, am I right?"

"Yeah. They're gone."

"Did they take or get rid of certain bodies?" she whispered.

"Shhh!" he said as his voice got intense. "I can't be sure. I haven't gone onto the grounds, so I don't know if they took *all* the bodies buried there- but I *am certain* they took the fat man and the dog. I've gone into the folly, but as to the rest- I just don't know." Q looked like the blood had gone from his face. This topic disturbed him deeply. "I'll tell you what, Gentry." slowly the blood returned, "I try not to think about that night- but it returns- in my dreams. I tried to tell myself the odd appearances I saw were visions of my imagination- but I never had an imagination before. The images are *so weird*. Did I see ghosts that night? Did you see them?"

Gentry could tell that now was not the time to tell Q that it wasn't his imagination. She tried to change the subject.

"The bodies, the boys bodies- I'm very curious to find out if he moved them or not. I mean I can't do anything with his diary if he's moved the bodies." her voice grew louder as she spoke, turning some of the people's heads nearby. Her face flushed pink.

148

"Let's go." she whispered and got up, Q followed as she walked out on the long wooden pier. When they were alone again, she continued.

"Do you remember the boys he had buried there? Or do you think that was all an illusion?"

"I do remember the boys. It's another thing I'm not sure about." Q rubbed his head where his bandages had been.

"Sorry about that." Gentry reached out to rub his head, but knocked too hard and hit his Boston Red Sox cap, making it fall to the ground. The demarcation line on his hairline had grown out severely, leaving a white stripe, like a skunk. She stopped, as they both did and picked it up and held it up to him. He immediately put it back on. Q looked irritated.

"Q," Gentry said, "You know that I know about your...your..."

"Just say it, god damn it! Albino!"

149

"I wasn't sure of a politically correct way to say that- but, as you say, albino. We both know about your being an albino, so the hell what? I don't care. Do you hear me? *I don't care!* Can't we get past that and go on?"

"Then why mention it at all?" he sounded furious.

"Because you looked so fucking mad back there when I accidentally hit your hat off- you damn tool!"

Q started to laugh once again. "You didn't just call me a 'tool', did you?"

Gentry looked at Q like he was the biggest goof she had ever met, then she joined him in laughing at herself.

"Right, I'm sorry." she said.

"I'm sorry, too."

They joined hands and continued to walk to the end of the pier. They enjoyed the breeze for nearly a minute before she continued.

"I kinda missed you." she said."

150

"Kinda missed you, too." he said, "Is that the only reason you came down here, the little boys I mean."

"Not really," she tried to lie, then went on. "I mean it was the main reason. I could have asked you about them on the phone I guess."

Q's eyes grew big and round. "So you wanted to see *me?*"

"No. Of course not." she answered and took her hand away from his. She had to remind herself that what she did *not* want was a relationship, *with anybody!*

"Oh." Q sounded deflated.

"How did you know that they were gone, aside from the fat man and the dog being gone?" she asked him sounding business like again.

"The castle was dark, it was night. I went into the folly and went up to the floor where we had left him, and he was gone. The dog, too. I looked towards the castle

151

through the window and it seemed eerie and void. At least, that was the feeling I got." he said as he looked off into the ocean, off towards Blake island. "I want to let you know that I moved my stash off that part of the island. I never want to go there again."

"Thanks for telling me that part- you didn't have to."

The stood looking over the edge of the pier, feeling the cold breeze tear right through them. The sun was going down, and she zipped up to the top of her jacket.

"I have to ask you to do me a favor- and it's hard for me to ask because I know that you don't owe me a thing- in fact, if anything- I owe you." she looked up at Q with seriousness in her eyes.

"What is it?" Q asked, then realization hit him. "Oh no- you're not going to ask me to go *back there?*"

"I have to! Yes, I need you to go back there, back to the castle. I need you to find out for sure if he's gone- and if the boys bodies are still there!"

"You don't mean that!" Q stammered.

"I have to know!" she begged, her eyes revealing her pain.

"Then *you* go! I'm done with that castle. You're trying to cast a play in hell, Gentry."

"Meaning?"

"Meaning there aren't any angels to play the parts- I'm no angel."

"I can live with that." she answered, "But I can't go now- it's too late. I would have to wait till tomorrow- I have plans that absolutely cannot wait."

"Oh, what- do am I keeping you from another date?" he said, jealousy starting to turn his stomach. He started to walk away.

"Damn you! Do you really think I'm like that? Do you?" Gentry was speechless.

153

"Why would I come down here and flirt with you if I had a boyfriend?"

"Don't you?" he stopped and turned towards her, "You were *flirting* with me?"

"Yes, NO!! I'm not like that at all. I came down here because I wanted to see you in person- talking on the phone wasn't enough. I had to see you."

"Why?" he asked, raising his voice an octave.

"Because. Isn't that enough?"

"No."

"It will have to be enough for now. I can't tell you how I feel until..." she stopped. This was what she didn't want to do.

"Until what?"

"Until I have this whole mess sorted out. Things about me...not you." her face was showing too much emotion, she covered her face with her hands.

154

Q walked back to her and grasped her by the hands. She squeezed his hands, he did the same.

"When do you want me to go?" he asked.

"Tonight. If possible. I know you have your dealings, but if you could go by tomorrow, I would be eternally grateful."

"Okay. I'll go tonight. Do you really have to be back in Bellingham tonight?"

"Yes. It's important. So is this, I know."

"I'll find out if the castle is deserted or not, but, I'm not going back inside the castle- I'll check the little graveyard-but like I said before, I *won't* go into the castle."

Gentry could tell he was serious, his eyes told of the terror that he knew.

"You won't have to. Find out if the bodies have been moved, if they are- like I think they are- you have to look

155

and see if there's any signs of life left."

"What a guy has to do these days." Q whispered into Gentry's ear.

She shot back and said, "What?"

"Nothing."

Gentry knew what he meant, but wanted to steer clear of the conversation that would certainly follow. There was a group of young men standing round the corner, and when Q and Gentry walked by they heard, "Hey Q! First comes love, then comes marria-"

"Shut up you fucking teabags!" Q angrily shouted back. Gentry gave him a curious look.

Q shrugged his shoulders, "Don't pay attention to them. They don't know what they're talking about."

"Walk me back to my bike." she said as they walked towards the parking lot with Q firmly in hand. Neither one wanted to say too much, so they continued to walk in

156

silence. Gentry was stoic and tried to maintain a rugged appearance as she put on her gloves and then her helmet. Q was going to kiss her, but she had on that 'don't even try' look on her face.

"I've got to go, Q. You have your promise to fulfill. I'll be counting on that."

"Will you come back tomorrow? You know, to find out about tonight?" he asked her with the faintest hope.

"I don't know. Perhaps I'll just call." she turned away, then she looked at Q and saw the eagerness in his eyes.

"Maybe. We'll see." she whispered.

Q was suddenly elated with her indecisiveness. "I think you will." he said with confidence.

"We'll see about that!" Gentry said with a look that resembled contempt.

Q shouted after her, "You'll be back!" then put his hands in his pocket and started whistling.

157

Chapter 13

Gentry rode though the freezing rain all the way back to Bellingham, and to Bryce's apartment. She rang the doorbell, Jecka answered.

"I had hoped it was you." Jecka said with her thick brown hair plaited down one side.

"We have to go right away- I have the strangest feeling." Gentry said as her stomach turned.

"Hell yeah!" Bryce's voice came from the bedroom, she was totally excited. "We're ready."

"But, we are not going to wake them, right?" Jecka said in her thick Romanian accent, as she wrung her sweater.

"No, we're not. But we are going to go inside the tunnels. I need to get some answers." Gentry shouted, "Let's go!"

"All for one and one for all- it's about mother fucking time!" Bryce said as she wheeled her way across the gravel to her van.

....

They finally arrived at the convent and parked outside
the wall surrounding the grounds so they wouldn't wake
the nuns.

"Jecka," Gentry asked, "You're sure they fall asleep by
8?"

"This time of the year, so close to Christmas especially,
yes I am sure."

Gentry was suddenly surprised- Christmas was
tomorrow! It hadn't even crossed her mind.

"Then they won't be awake for us, it's 10:30."

"They will be asleep. They always sleep soundly." Jecka
was biting her bottom lip, she was worried.

"Finally, a little bit of excitement!" Bryce said with
vigor.

"Bryce," Gentry said in a voice that was stern, but quiet,

160

"Remember, we have to be quiet. All will be ruined if we wake them."

"Oh yeah, right!" she said giving her a little salute.

"Come this way to the back, around the side of the convent. It's quieter than coming straight on." Jecka whispered.

Quietly they tiptoed and wheeled round the convent, stopping intermittently to make sure they had not been discovered. Once they made their way out from behind the convent and they were sure that they had made their way in silence, Gentry took the copies of the plans from her backpack, the copies of the tunnels and unrolled them while Jecka held the flashlight.

"The tunnels go all through the convent and they come out there." Gentry pointed to a big evergreen tree 100 yards straight out back. Slowly they went over to the tree and circled around, poking through the ground, but they

161

could not find an entrance.

"That's odd," Gentry said, "Should've been right here! I don't see a thing!"

"Maybe it's *under* the grass." Bryce said as she started to wheel her way around the tree.

"Being here gives me chills." Jecka chimed in.

"Chills?" Gentry asked.

"Yes. This is where I saw that ghost, the horrible ghost I told you about."

The world seemed to take a few steps back. Gentry got a gleam in her eyes. "The ghost with the hood?"

"Yes."

"Oh my god!" Gentry suddenly yelled.

"What is it, G? What's the matter?" Bryce asked. She knew when something was bothering Gentry.

"My god, my god!" she repeated as she started walking around knocking on the ground as she went. "I don't

162

fucking believe it!"

"What the fuck?" Bryce insisted on knowing.

"Jecka wasn't seeing ghosts- she was seeing my sister!"

"What?!" Jecka and Bryce said at the same time.

"Jecka told me about a ghost she had seen a few times
before- but it can't have been a ghost- it was my sister!
They let her out for exercise, through these tunnels. Those
fucking sisters kept my sister, they never did put her up
for adoption-*they kept her!*"

She was like an animal, on her knees searching
desperately for the metal lid. Finally she found the lid but
it was locked with a stick pushed through the lock hole on
the latch. She quickly pushed the stick out. She opened
the door to a crypt that was narrow down the ladder, but
opened up wide at the bottom.

"Why would they keep her? Why wouldn't they put her
up for adoption the same as you?" Bryce was shaking her

head.

"Who would do this?" Jecka asked.

"It had to be Catherine and Mary Alice. Those two had secrets to hide. They wanted to keep my sister for themselves- I don't know how, I don't know why. Maybe they were afraid of being found out- even to the point of hiding her after their deaths!" Gentry was furious.

"But Sister Mary Alice died months ago, and Catherine only days ago." Jecka cried out.

"Are you coming down with me, Jecka?" she nodded her head. "Sorry Bryce, you'll have to be the lookout."

"I know," Bryce said, "*Go!*"

Slowly Gentry and Jecka made their way into the tunnel. It was dark, the only light coming from the flashlight that Gentry held. Long and narrow at first, but it began to spread out as they walked along.

"This place is filthy!" Gentry said as she continued

164

walking down the tunnel.

Angling down they followed the tunnel, stopping and looking at the catacombs beneath the earth. The tunnel was a labyrinth, with three ways to travel. One way was filled with skeletons set up crypt style in the walls, lying down as if to rest, rather than for eternal sleep. They looked at the map Gentry had copied and she realized that much more had been made of the tunnel since it's inception.

"Look here," Gentry started, "these parts of the tunnel aren't even on this map. They must have been built since this map was made."

"How old do you think it is?"

"Don't know. Hard to read with this flashlight. It's so dark." she said as she walked down the catacombs.

"This is eerie."

"I am scared." Jecka shuddered.

165

"They're just skeletons. They're not alive anymore."

"Still." Jecka came up to Gentry and grabbed her arm.

"I don't think we'll find anything down this way. Let's go back."

"Okay."

They walked back to the entrance of the tunnel and went down the middle way. The tunnels second entrance was not only dusty, but filled with rat feces and spider webs. The smell was horrendous.

"Doesn't look like anyone's been down this way either."

"How can you tell?"

"There's no human footprints, the dust hasn't been moved for years." she said as she turned back once more.

"This is the last way. Let's try once more."

Gentry and Jecka walked down the tunnel with the flashlight going from side to side.

"This way looks like it has been walked through

recently...this must be the way."

As they continued to walk they noticed worn out and torn furniture against the walls. First there was the sofa, it was worn and dirty, Gentry's anger began to rise as she threw up her hands.

"I can't believe this filth! How could the nuns stand it?"

"Most of us were surviving- I know I was." Jecka said.

"You weren't hiding my sister- they were!"

Gentry's eyes finally rested on a little desk, it was small and filled with pictures hand drawn of the trees and squirrels that lived here in the forest. She walked immediately walked over and picked them up and was looking through them, trying to make sense out of what she saw.

"This is the place I saw in the super 8 movies, but why did they film this?"

She looked around the desk for some clue-was somebody

living here now?

"This must be from when they had my sister living here! They must have put her up for adoption when she was older, but why would they keep her down here in these filthy fucking tunnels? I wouldn't put a dog in conditions like these, let alone a human being!"

"Keep the light in one place- I'm getting dizzy." Jecka said.

"We're going to find out why they did this. Let's go to the other end of this tunnel to make some sense of this- let's see what's out there. Supposedly, the map shows that the tunnel goes into the convent around the back door."

"But Gentry, that's where we moved the iron bars- from when you broke me out of the convent. There can't be a secret door, or we'd have found it that day!"

They ran toward the opposite end and found the access leading up to convents secret door- it had been pushed on

168

by the iron bars they had moved there, and between them they were able to make a break in the doorway about ½ inch wide. Gentry could see that it did come up and became a secret entry right behind the large statue of Christ in the chapel. Gentry also could see how it was hidden, and kept out of view by it's location.

"I can see inside of the chapel, this is where it empties into the convent."

"Let's get inside and I'll take you to the place I think the adoption papers would be." Jecka was scared, not only for the odd sights she had seen in the tunnel, but for the nuns- she was frightened were going to make her stay. "I'll show you, then I am going back with Bryce. I'm so scared."

"Oh," Gentry let out a groan, "First you're going to help me with this door. Show me where you think the papers are, then go wait for me."

They both had to push with all their weight to get the

door open against the iron bars pushed into place last time they were here. Finally with a quiet rumble, the door opened, and they both walked inside. The convent was dark and the only shadows on the walls were the ones they made now with the flashlight. Jecka led Gentry to the room where the sisters gathered round the fire,only there was no fire now, only embers glowing red.

"There's a vault, behind what looks like the wall there." She pointed. "That's where they put my papers." Jecka walked up to the wall and with a push, it clicked and it opened wide. "Can I go now?"

"Yeah. Get out of here quick." Gentry took the key from around her neck and put it in the lock- it worked! She was there for a long moment when she found her adoption papers, which she promptly put into her pocket. She searched to find another set of adoption papers, but to her dismay she didn't find a single other set. She looked through once again and thought,

I know it must be here! My adoption papers are right here- Where can they have put my sisters?

Then, she found Jecka's papers. She looked at them quickly, then made an astonishing discovery! She would look at this later, as she took a third look for adoption papers before giving up. She locked the vault so the nuns would be none the wiser. She turned and the light fell on Jecka, standing there shivering.

"I thought you went back- I thought you were afraid?"

"I was. But I thought I would have enough courage to come back and at least be your lookout."

"Let's go back to the tunnels, and look there once more."

Jecka took the flashlight from Gentry and walked ahead, until they came to the secret door where the tunnel began.

Suddenly, Gentry had an epiphany!

"We have to push our way through the door, with both

of our weights, right?"

"That's right."

"Then if a person was small, they wouldn't be able to push their way through."

Jecka nodded.

"Jecka," Gentry said, "I think I made a horrible mistake taking you from here."Gentry's lips were quivering, her world taking on a grotesque hue.

"What?" Jecka shockingly asked, "You were sent by God! You saved me."

"But what did I have to do to save you?" Gentry took the flashlight from Jecka and down the secret staircase. Side to side she made the flashlight glow onto the skeletons in the catacombs. She went back to the small desk and saw a moldy, old half eaten loaf of bread next to a copy of *The Collected Works of Emily Dickinson,* the one that had come into Gentry's mind more than once before. She held

172

it tenderly in her arms.

"Jecka," Gentry wanted to cry, "I did a terrible thing when I was here before."

"What did you do?"

"I pushed the irons onto the door. I think that was the only way she had to get out."

"Who?"

"My sister."

Chapter 14

Gentry turned her light around the room until it fell upon a small bundle laying on the floor. She squinted, then it became apparent as to what is was, the profile of a body. She felt the blood drain from her head, from her whole body as she began to scream, *"OH, no, no, no!"* she fell to her knees. The room was spinning round and round, she couldn't think straight.

"That is *the* ghost!" Jecka said in a horrified voice, putting her hand over her mouth.

"This isn't a ghost- *it is my sister!"* as fast as she said it she was on the floor turning the small bony body towards her. She looked dreadfully thin and tiny, and her arms had been unspeakable deformed- one being of usual length and the other but a hand coming out like a stalk of corn from her shoulder. Her head was covered by the hood that had been put there by the sister, *how could they cover her up?*

How?

When Gentry lifted the hood she saw what kind of vile joke god could play on a person. The left side of her head was not there, it was just gone! The tiny body had a few shreds of hair, and her skin had the texture of boils. She couldn't have weighed more than 60 pounds. Gentry's weeps turned into ghastly moans. Her blood ran up to her head, then ran back out. It was as if she could feel the liquid in her veins congeal. Jecka ran back to the entrance of the tunnel, her eyes were becoming used to the absence of light. She ran to tell Bryce what had transpired in the moments before. Bryce was shocked but told Jecka that they should leave her to do her own grieving, at least for now, they would keep watch.

Gentry slowly looked up as she heard a sound. It was the grim reaper. He spoke, "Now your sister, your *real sister*

176

has died. Are you going to go through with this?" He stood there before her, an invisible wind blew open his cloak, underneath his cloak was a skeleton, standing there, smiling his toothy grin.

She looked at him through tears, then said, "What am I supposed to do? Pretend like this never happened?"

"Yes. Exactly."

"You know I could never do that."

"Then I must tell you; I will see you again- soon."

"Are you coming for me?"

"No."

"Aren't you curious where I will appear?"

"Not particularly."

"Romania. It's a beautiful country, for some."

"Tell me one more thing." she looked at him with no fear.

"What is it?"

177

"Where do those suck holes in the cemetery lead?"

"I'm really not at liberty to say- I have my secrets. I can tell you any spirit that goes in, *won't* be back again." then the wind blew him away in pieces.

Gentry hugged her sister one last time, and felt the presence of a small whistle around her neck. She removed it and put it in her pocket.

When Gentry finally came out, it must have been half an hour, Bryce asked, "G, I'm sorry about your sister. Couldn't she get out? Or at least call for help when no one came to feed her?"

"She did call for help. Only no one knew what that noise was- they probably thought, like Jecka- that it was a ghost." Gentry pulled out a whistle from her pocket and held it up for them to see.

"There never was a ghost. There was only a child trying to whistle for help. I was afraid to help her." Jecka said as

178

she turned her head and started sobbing.

Gentry started walking towards the van. Bryce and Jecka called out, "You're not going to leave her here?"

"There's nothing I can do for her now. I can't even bury her without everybody fucking in my business! *What in the hell were we doing here, Bryce, Jecka? What? Let the dead bury the dead- I've had enough!*"

Bryce looked at Jecka with a strange glance, then started following Gentry to the van. Gentry started crying again, angered with herself when she thought of her poor sister being locked in from the outside by a stick, and from the inside by iron bars that she herself had put in position. *Stupid Fucking idiot!!* She imagined that the little girl, actually little woman, died thinking that no one cared. One person did care, and now she was after the only person left to answer- the evil man who had started it all.

……...

Chapter 15

The three girls were driving back to Bryce's apartment- it had been quiet as a tomb. Gentry spoke, "Jecka," she said with her eyes swollen from tears, "when I was in the vault I noticed your papers and I pulled them out."

"Oh, thank you. I never thought I'd see them again. They took my passport, did you get it-*yes!*" Jecka put out her hand as if Gentry would put them there.

"You never told me that your *real last name was Baumann, and you're Jewish!*"

"You never asked me. Yes, that is my real name, and yes, I am Jewish!" Jecka innocently told Gentry.

"You had a sister, right? Much older, sister if I'm not mistaken." Gentry stroked her chin as if she was a modern day Sherlock Holmes.

All the wheels in her head were turning now.

181

"Yes. I had a much older sister, her name was...."

"Ruth! Her name was Ruth. She came to America a long time ago; then you lost touch with her, right again?"

"Yes. That is correct. We never heard from her again. But I don't understand what all this is leading to." Jecka's brow was starting to sweat.

"Your brother and mother never told you what happened, did they?" her voice getting louder.

"Now you're scaring me!"

"Unfucking real!"she shouted.

"G! What the hell? You're scaring me, too. How did you know about her sister?" Bryce said.

"Because that was the name of *my mother!!*"

Bryce and Jecka gasped. That would be incredible, almost impossible!

"How could my sister be your mother? That would make you my...my..."

182

"Niece. I would be your niece." Gentry said as if all the wind had been knocked out of her.

"But how do you know that? Surely it doesn't say in the papers you received..."

"I know because the man who told me he was my father told me her name. Ruth Baumann."

"Whoa! WTF! You found your *father?*" Bryce shouted.

"Yeah, see? Now you both know my fucking business." Gentry covered her face and although you couldn't see it- you could tell it was horribly distorted with anguish.

"SORRY!" Bryce was back to being angry. "But why wouldn't you want friends to know that you found your father? Tell me that, shithead!"

"Because now that you know- you'll want to know more. I can't tell you more...not now, not yet; probably not ever."

"Tell me everything! I mean it G! I want the whole story!" Bryce leaned over as she was driving and the van

183

started to roll to one side. She righted it fast.

"Okay. So you won't go freaking nuts and kill us all- I'll tell you as much as I can. But I can't tell you all you'll want to know."

On the ride back to Bryce's apartment, Gentry told them as much as she could, but she did not tell them about the boys buried in her cemetery or about the wicked demon who was her father. They planned and plotted all night long as to what was to happen next. This was all to happen, there was no way of getting around a problem of this enormity. At least she knew the origins of her mother's skull, so it was one less thing she had to do.

Chapter 16

Gentry had fallen asleep on Bryce's couch and had fitful dreams that night. When she woke the next morning she had wanted to go without seeing Bryce and Jecka, but that was not to be. Gentry was getting dressed when Bryce came into the room.

"What are you going to do now? This morning?"

"I have to drive to Seattle. I'll be back in a few hours."

"To see Q?"

"Yes." she said as she turned her head away. Bryce wasn't going to give her a hard time now, was she?

"I'm going to look on the web for tickets while you're gone." Bryce said it like it was agreed that she was going.

"For who?"

"For all of us. You, me and Jecka. You got her passport back, didn't you?"

185

"Yeah, so?"

"I thought we all agreed- we're going to go to Romania- it's the place where you thought he might go- to the Carpathian mountains." Bryce sounded firm.

"Yes, but Bryce- *I* said *I* would go- not the three of us!" Gentry said.

"No matter! I know Jecka wants to go- she feels responsible, somehow. And I know that I'm going to go to keep an eye on you." Bryce said with a wink.

"I don't need a babysitter, Bryce- and as for Jecka, I can't take her and be responsible for her, too!" *Damn it!*

"*We are going- all three of us!* Get used to it."

"I've got to go. I'll be back in town in a few hours." she said as she walked out the door and slammed it shut.

God damn her, and Jecka! I don't need them tugging at my conscience!

....

On this Christmas day the usual was to be expected- traffic was heavy on the road early in the morning, but Gentry could go in and out with her motorcycle. Slush was accumulating, but drivable. She parked and walked back to pier 55, but again did not see Q.

"Guess who?" Q stepped out of the shadows. Gentry was tired and not in the mood- but she managed a smile.

"Q." she said.

"I wasn't sure if you were going to make it." Q said trying to fit the puzzle pieces together- she was so *quirky.*

"Well, what did you find out?" she asked.

"You were right! No one is living at the castle, not a single soul. You were also right about the bodies being moved- I don't know where they are, but they are gone."

"God damn him! Jesus Christ!" she said to the heavens.

"So, I guess you're done, right? I mean, you don't know where he might be- am I right?" he asked trying to look

187

into her eyes, but she was not looking at him- she was looking across, at Blake island.

"I'm *not* done. I have a place to look-but it's far away."

"Really? Where?"

"What the fuck do you want to know for? It's *not* your problem!" she looked right at him, into his eyes. Her eyes were burning hot, but all he saw was pain. He put his arms around her and she didn't have the strength to fight him off. Gentry tried to put her hands between them, but she was tired of everything. She let him hold her.

"I'm going to go to Romania. My friends Bryce and Jecka are coming along- what the fuck for- I don't know."

"When are you leaving?" Q whispered into her ear.

"Soon. Soon." her exhaustion was evident.

Time seemed to go by as they stood there. "Merry Christmas, by the way." he said as he pulled out a wrapped gift box. Gentry's jaws dropped, "I had forgotten

188

it was Christmas. Thank you, Q. I don't have a present for you."

"That's not what Christmas is for- it's supposed to be about giving, not receiving."

Gentry looked at Q once again- and it seemed like it was the very first time. He was being romantic! *Or maybe he just seemed that way.* She had no way of knowing.

Gentry opened the box and there was a ring-not an engagement ring- but a ring, none-the-less. She looked at the stone that was encased in the ring, then she looked at Q with a curious glance.

"I don't understand- what is this supposed to be?" she asked.

"It's a ring I had made from the stone of the castle- I thought you might like it- as a remembrance of me." Q said, "Look, take it out and put it on."

"Wait. I can't accept a ring from you, Q. I..."

189

"It's *not* an engagement ring! It's a *ring.* It doesn't mean anything except I thought you would like it- I had it made special- for you." Q explained.

Gentry put it on and spread her fingers- he was right. The ring looked spectacular.

"And you say you had it made, especially for me? When did you get the stone? Not last night?"

"Naw. I got it when I was moving my stash off the island. I took some stone that had fallen from the building. I had it made then." Q was a bit embarrassed to have to explain about the ring, but he knew that she wouldn't take the ring until she knew the details.

"I don't know what to say, except to say thank you, Q- it was sweet of you."

"Now don't go saying that around here- what I don't need is to get the reputation of being 'sweet'." he started chucking under his breath. She joined in his laughter and

190

said, "No, I won't. It will be our secret, k?"

"Pinky swear?" he said as he put his little finger out.

"*Pinky swear?* What are we, 12?" but she put her pinky finger to his and they swore it would be a secret.

She now felt a little better, but she was still upset because of last night. Gentry wasn't sure if she was going to tell Q or not. Instead, she changed the subject.

"Did you have any trouble last night? No one bothered you?" she said.

"No. No one. I am more worried with your going to Romania. How do you know he will be there? More important, how do you know you'll okay if you do meet him again?" his voice sounding deep with concern.

Gentry took a look at the ring once more before she put her gloves back on her hands. She shoved the box into her pocket.

"You don't need to stress about my going. I'm good at

taking care of myself. Besides, I have the advantage now-
I know he's a prideful, hateful man. I know how to deal
with that."

"Gentry," he began, "How is knowing *that* going to stop
him once he has access to you? He still has that gruesome
lady and the skinny man to help him. You're going to be
walking into a trap!" he grabbed her by the hands.

"Q, last night was terrible. I found out how far this man
would go. I found my sister last night." she said as the
blood drained away to leave her face a frightening white.

"That's good, isn't it?" he looked at her face and felt it
was wrong. "Isn't it?"

"No, Q. I found her dead." her lips were trembling and
he felt her start to fall.

"No, Gentry- no!" he grabbed her tight once more but
this time she rejected him.

"Like I said, it's not your problem!" she shoved him

back.

"Like hell it's not! I care about you, Gentry. It is *my* problem!" his face changed from rage to anger although you could hardly see a difference.

"You told me what you found out- that's enough. I don't want you to care about me. I'm not worth it." she started to cry as Q put his arms around her one more time. Gentry was not going to get away that easily.

"Then we deserve each other," he said lifting up her chin with his fingers. "We're both oddballs. We don't fit in."

"We're totally different! We want different things out of life- you know this." she said. Gentry started to walk away when Q yelled out, "Gentry," he started, "I want to go with you when you go to Romania!"

"No! I don't want you to go. I don't want anyone to go- you, Bryce, or Jecka!" she started to run. Q chased her.

Finally he caught up to her. He grabbed her by the arm

193

and turned her back towards him.

"Listen to me!" he began, "I know that you don't want me- not now anyway. But you'll need me over there and you know it."

"I don't *know* that! How can you even say that? I'm leaving." She yanked back her arm and continued to her motorcycle. While she was putting on her helmet Q thought it was worth one more try.

"Listen to me, Gentry!" he began, "I do remember that night- all of it. I remember seeing ghosts, which is why I think your avoiding me- because you saw them, too! Am I right? And I guess that it's not the first time you've seen ghosts, because you talked to the spirits of the little boys. NO ONE who sees ghosts for the first time would actually try to talk to them." she continued getting ready to take off.

He reached over and took her key out of the ignition. "I'm

194

right, aren't I?"

Gentry knew he was right, and that was part of the reason she didn't want him to come along. Her feelings were spent.

"Q," she began, "you're right, partly." she lifted off her helmet and put out her hand for Q to place her keys. He did.

"What is the other reason?" Q had the look of urgency in his eyes.

"The other reason is,- man, you're going to think I'm lame."

"Tell me!"

"Holy freakin shit!" she said inaudibly. "If you remember back at the castle- everything that happened that night- then you'll remember my telling you how things were complicated between Katie and myself."

"I do. I remember saying that if we ever got out of there,

195

maybe you could tell me." Q rested his hand on hers.

"Well, we're out of there. I've never told this to anyone, not even Bryce, my best friend." she admitted. "A couple years ago- the same night that Bryce had her horrible accident, actually-Katie and her friends wanted to play a dirty joke on me. Which they did."

"What happened Gentry?" Q asked, "What did they do to you?"

Gentry's voice started cracking. This was harder to do than she imagined. "They had this guy, who I truly believed liked me, man- I was so naive. They had him take me out on a date."

He prodded her on. "And?"

"It was all a scam, they had it all planned. He drugged me at dinner, then he took me out to the woods where he raped me- not *just* raped me, but he savagely, and brutally attacked me. He beat me senseless, then left me for dead."

"Oh my god." he said unbelievably.

"OMG is right, only that wasn't the end of it."

"What else did they do to you?" Q was angry.

"Katie and her friends were all watching- watching and laughing at me when it happened. I've never felt so humiliated- so vulnerable and raw. They wouldn't help me, all they wanted to do was dehumanize me, which they did, very dehumanized, and violated." she started to sob quietly, she started to heave until Q put his arms around her. "That was my first time; and my last...I can't trust people- I can't trust in you."

Q was miserable about what Gentry had told him, but he had hope.

"Gentry," he began, "I think I understand. I know that you've been put into a position of distrust, but I want to prove you wrong. I want to show you that you *can* believe in me, that you can have confidence in me!"

"I don't think you can, very frankly." she wiped her tears.

"You have to give me a chance!" he took her hands in his and tenderly kissed them.

"Let me go with you to Romania- not to prove this to you, but to give you male protection- I hear that Central Europe is rough, you practically *need* to have a man with your party, particularly to sidestep those white slavery rings. I hear they're big right now. "

"You don't have any money to go to Europe, or passport." she said.

"Money? If that's all you're worried about let me tell you that *I have money!* I'll even pay for your ticket- how's that? And I have my passport, I have to go to Canada all the time- so don't give me grief about nothing!" he said with veracity.

"Shit, shit...shit!" slipped out of her mouth. She gave Q one of her *I'm not in any mood* looks, then backed off slowly. "I think you're right about that Europe freaking

protocol - I have heard some stories about Romania, from

an actual Romanian!"

"Then I'm going with you, right?" the suspense was

killing him when she finally said, "Okay. You can come

along with us- might as well take one more." she said

mockingly. "But you have to promise to stay back when I

find him- I want to face him alone."

"Uh uh." he said as his head shook from side to side.

"There's no way I'm going to let you fight him alone."

"Okay," she smiled, "I'm not going to argue about that

here. It's a future fight. I've gotta go. I still have to deal

with some dead people back home." she gave him a quick

kiss on the cheek, he smiled. She pulled her helmet up

and yelled back to him, "Merry Christmas, Q." and she

drove off for home.

199

<u>Chapter 17</u>

Gentry pulled up to her back door and sneaked in to hear her parents and Katie having a great time for Christmas. She felt the empty feeling that usually accompanied their celebrations and she went straight to her room, positive that she would not be missed. It was still light out as it was not quite 5 o'clock, she decided to head for the kitchen and make a cup of cocoa. She sat down at the kitchen table when Katie came into the room.

"Hey Gentry."

"Hey." Gentry said without a lot of cheer, this was not what she was in the mood for.

"You didn't join us, I didn't know if you wanted to have a Christmas dinner with us, we had it about an hour ago."

"Whoopee!" she deadpanned.

"I know we haven't been close sisters, or any kind of

sisters, actually."

"*REALLY?* I hadn't noticed." sarcasm dripping from her voice.

"I had hoped that this could be the start of a family for us." she put a small box in front of Gentry.

"What's this?" Gentry asked.

"Merry Christmas." Katie said, she sounded sincere.

"I'm not in the mood." she said as she pushed it back. "I don't want anything from you."

"Look," Katie's eyes started to tear up, "I know that mom's attitude has been particularly nasty ever since you brought me home."

"Ya think?"

"I'm not sure of all that happened to me- and you probable don't care much- I know that if our places were switched that I wouldn't even try."

"So why are you even trying?" she snapped.

202

"Because I remember some of what happened. At least I think I do. Or maybe I don't, it could be the drugs he put into me, or the drugs that they've put into me since I've been rescued. But I *do* remember you came and *you* saved me." Katie sat down at the kitchen table next to Gentry.

"Then let's just shake hands and call it complete." Gentry said as she finished her cocoa. She looked at Katie with her cynicism intact.

"But I thought- since we talked that night, that we were starting to work things out. I thought we were becoming friends." Katie reached for Gentry's hand.

"Are you being this way because mom's treating you bad?"

Gentry got up from the table, slammed down her empty cup and yelled, "*NO!* That's not why-Yeah, mom has always treated me badly but that's *nothing, nothing do you hear me,* compared to what you have done to me!!"

Katie put her hands to her mouth, feeling as if she was

kicked in the gut by Gentry. She couldn't breathe.

"Merry Christmas!" Gentry said in a most scornful way,

picking up the present and flung it against the wall,

stomping out of the room leaving Katie sobbing at the

kitchen table.

. . . .

Chapter 18

That night Gentry was in her room packing for the trip to Romania. Bryce, Jeka and Q were all going with her, but that's not what she was thinking about. Right now all she could think about was what she was going to do with Manion before she left for Bucharest. She knew she could count on the boys in the cemetery and Sir Alfie, the eldest boy in their part of the children's graveyard.

She had reached a decision about what she was going to do; now all she had to do was put the plan into action.

When it grew darker Gentry was out for blood. She put on her heaviest jacket and went out from the front of her family's house and tiptoed to the back of the cemetery- she was going to make sure Manion didn't see her coming. She had whispered to the boys and Alfie as to what was going to happen and when she was positive they knew part that they were to play in the melee, she was ready.

She walked up to the angel statue where Mrs. Manion had always been and found her poking her head in and out of burial plots.

"Manion!"

"Oh! You startled me, dear. What is it, I'm busy." Manion said as she continued.

"I have information for you."

"Oh! My, my...I knew you would come around. So, where are they buried?"

"Well you know they aren't buried here, in this cemetery." Gentry politely said.

"Yes...yes. I know! But where are they buried?" Manion desperately asked.

"I did some more digging, *no offense*- I even went over to their cemetery and I checked them out, or at least I *tried* to check them out." she said kindly, but you could tell there was more buried in her voice.

"What does that mean? Did you or didn't you see them?" Manion had tears in her eyes.

"I saw their headstones," Gentry started to walk backwards, Manion followed. "But I'm afraid their spirits had already flown away-*fsssssh!* Gone!"

"That can't be true! That is not true! I don't believe you...you bloody little bitch!" Manion screamed at her.

"But there was a lady, a lady dressed in green who *was* there. She had a message for you." Gentry's voice was titillating as she walked, enough so that Manion continued to follow her behind the mausoleum.

"What kind of message could *she* have?" Manion was floating close by.

"The message was from your ex-husband." you could hear her footsteps coming closer.

"She said that he warned you to stay away from him and

the boys- or he would have you taken by Satan to live in hell forever!" she said with enthusiasm.

"How could he do that? He can't make me go to hell, or anywhere else, for that matter."

"No, you're probably right. But I'll bet no one ever told you to go to the *Hole.* "

"The hole?" she questioned with one elderly eyebrow extending up.

"Yes. We're here now."

"I don't see a thing. You are trying to trick me."

"You're probably right again. I can't even push you in- even if there was a hole." Gentry made sure the hole was squarely between her and Mrs. Manion.

"That's right! You can't."

"But that doesn't mean you *can't* be pushed in-"Gentry startled Manion with her sudden scream, *"NOW!"*

Alfie and the boys jumped out of the bushes and pushed

208

a sudden screaming Manion into the hole and *whosh!*

She was being pulled in and tried to grab Finn by the

collar. Sir Alfie and the other boys pulled Finn back, all

the boys grabbed his feet and pulled harder than they

thought they could. Manions grip was firm but the boys

held on with an unyielding strength. Her voice was at a

terrifying pitch, she yelled, "You sick, twisted fucks!"

Then, as fast as she had grabbed Finn's garment, she

released his collar with a loud 'snap'. It was followed by a

whoosh, then instant silence. Sir Alfie and the boys took a

step back, and took a big sigh of relief.

"I had me doubts- but I think we got her!" Sir Alfie said.

"Are you okay, Finn?" Gentry looked at his wretched

little face, he was terrified. "You gave your all- you all

did- Thank you so much!"

"I was so afraid, I thought I would pass out!" Finn said

looking sickly yellow.

"Are you sure she's gone? She can't come back, can she?" Randy asked.

"Well, Alfie?"

"I can be certain of this- though I have never known about these *holes* for long- I hereby decree that she never take a step in this cemetery again!" Sir Alfie took off his phoney crown and held it over his head and cheered. The boys did what Alfie did, and cheered alongside him.

Gentry was relieved, and that's about all she felt. She had Mrs. Manion heaved out and she would find out where the holes lead- she had asked the grim reaper but he was no help- she felt a little bit better, but she needed her hot cup of cocoa.

Chapter 19

A couple weeks later when the four companions were on the plane heading for Bucharest, Gentry was deep in thought. Jecka was sitting with Bryce up in front of the plane, while Gentry and Q sat directly behind them. Gentry was busy showing Q her medallion, the charm that the evil man had thrown onto her mother's dying body.

"See? Here, in the back of the charm- there is a Romanian warning, to ward off evil."

"So between this charm, and the fact that your mother and this girl sitting in front of me are related- that's why we're going to Romania?" Q asked.

"Not exactly. That's not all." she knew that now would be a good time to tell Q her entire history.

"Q," she started, "there's way more to tell you about

myself. I wasn't sure I would ever do that, but since you're coming along with us, I feel I should tell you now."

"Go on." Q said as he grasped her hands. His hands were warm, but her hands were cold and clammy.

"That night, on the island- I was talking with the boys we both saw." she paused. Q went on looking at her.

"I've always been able to communicate with spirits of the dead- ghosts."

"Come on! That's not possible!" Q stammered. He didn't believe her.

"It's true!" she said, "I knew you wouldn't believe me- no one ever does; not that I've told a lot of people- they would have me committed."

"How could people believe you? I mean you're talking like one of those 'psychics'- I mean it's just not possible." he continued.

"See? It's useless. I finally get the nerve up to tell

212

someone I care about this- and boom! You think I'm crazy."

"You *care* about me?" Q was caught off guard and pleasantly surprised.

"I didn't mean *that.* " she tried to backpeddle.

"No! You did mean *that!* I heard you plain as day." he smiled at her.

"What's the point? You don't believe me. So I think..."

"The point is that I will *try to believe you.* That's what people do when they care about each other." he grasped her hand again and kissed the back of them.

"So, you care about me?" Gentry asked with a bit of sarcasm. It was hard for her to believe that anyone could.

"Yeah, I do. I've cared for quite a while." Q said with her hand interlaced with his.

"I don't want us to start making mistakes over this- I want you to understand that point."

213

"We won't. I promise."

"I mean it, Q. It's like that saying 'Those who do not learn from history are doomed to repeat it.' If history teaches us anything it's this- When you care about another person, you're more liable to make mistakes protecting that person from danger!" she said in low tone of voice so that the girls wouldn't hear them.

"You're one crazy be-otch, Gentry." he whispered, "but I think I could fall for you."

"Then understand this- I could never fall for you, *ever!* Whatever happens- happens." she tried to let go of his hands, but he would not let go.

Right now Gentry was trying to figure out what they were going to do when they landed. And where in Romania they were going to find the despised immortal infidel.

Made in the USA
Charleston, SC
02 September 2011